"Are you sure you're okay?"

"You don't need to keep asking that, all right?"

"Yeah." Wyatt relented. "Sorry." But he wasn't about to admit defeat and leave. There had to be something he could do. "Wait…are you leaving?"

Marilyn shook her head no, but he didn't believe it. It only told him that if she was leaving, it wasn't by choice.

"Come push us on the swings!" one of the twins called from the yard.

Wyatt held up a hand that he'd heard them. "In a minute, okay?" He turned toward Marilyn. He let women come and go in and out of his life with practiced ease, so the sharp prick at the thought of losing her and the girls startled him. He reached his hand toward her elbow. "Mari, please. Tell me what's going on."

She pulled in the smallest of breaths, and after a half second of connection he knew they both felt, she pulled away.

This weird protective thing? This "you can't hurt her" battle ~~~~~~~~~~~~~~~~~~~~~~~e?

It stumpe~~~~~~~~~~~~~~~~~~~~~~~~~~ken carousels

Allie Pleiter, an award-winning author and RITA® Award finalist, writes both fiction and nonfiction. Her passion for knitting shows up in many of her books and all over her life. Entirely too fond of French macarons and lemon meringue pie, Allie spends her days writing books and avoiding housework. Allie grew up in Connecticut, holds a BS in speech from Northwestern University and lives near Chicago, Illinois.

Books by Allie Pleiter

Love Inspired

Wander Canyon

Their Wander Canyon Wish

Matrimony Valley

His Surprise Son
Snowbound with the Best Man
Wander Canyon Courtship

Blue Thorn Ranch

The Texas Rancher's Return
Coming Home to Texas
The Texan's Second Chance
The Bull Rider's Homecoming
The Texas Rancher's New Family

Visit the Author Profile page at Harlequin.com for more titles.

Their Wander
Canyon Wish

Allie Pleiter

LOVE INSPIRED
INSPIRATIONAL ROMANCE

LOVE INSPIRED®
INSPIRATIONAL ROMANCE

Recycling programs
for this product may
not exist in your area.

ISBN-13: 978-1-335-48796-4

Their Wander Canyon Wish

Copyright © 2020 by Alyse Stanko Pleiter

This edition published by arrangement with Harlequin Books S.A.

For questions and comments about the quality of this book, please contact us at CustomerService@Harlequin.com.

Love Inspired
22 Adelaide St. West, 40th Floor
Toronto, Ontario M5H 4E3, Canada
www.Harlequin.com

Printed in U.S.A.

But they that wait upon the Lord shall renew their strength; they shall mount up with wings as eagles; they shall run, and not be weary; and they shall walk, and not faint.

—*Isaiah* 40:31

In memory of Bella.
Writing partner, coffee companion
and quite simply the Best Dog Ever.

Chapter One

Out of order?

Seriously?

Marilyn Sofitel couldn't believe the sign hanging from the large closed door in front of her. In all the years she'd grown up in Wander Canyon, the carousel had never been out of order. The whimsical, dollar-a-ride merry-go-round was the town's pride and joy, the unofficial symbol of the tiny Colorado community. Housed in a big red round barn in the center of town, it was the one thing she could always count on to be there.

Not today. How could the carousel be broken? And on today of all days, when her girls had been clamoring for a ride and she'd finally made the time to give them one?

Her daughter Maddie scowled at the closed door. "Aw. Why's it shut, Mom?"

Margie, Maddie's twin, squinted at the handwritten words inked messily onto a scrap of wood. She tugged on Marilyn's sleeve and looked up. "What's that say?" At six and a half, the girls were starting to read, constantly pointing out and asking about words. Usually she took joy in their eagerness to read. Not this particular moment.

Marilyn tried to keep the frustration out of her voice as she pointed to each of the words. "It says 'Out of Order.'"

"What's that mean?" Maddie said, her jutting lower lip telling Marilyn she'd already guessed.

Marilyn's chest sank at the idea of disappointing her girls. "It means the carousel is broken." After a sad second she added, "Today, at least," as an attempt at optimism.

She'd been an optimist once. A starry-eyed young woman who chose to see the best in everyone and every situation. And now, here she was, back in Wander Canyon with no idea of her future and two daughters who wouldn't get to ride the carousel today.

She fought the urge to groan. Or cry. Or both. Today was a beautiful June Thursday, the day she'd chosen to be her first day of a new start. The day she was dropping off her first resumé to start the search for a part-time job. What did it say that she couldn't get even this tiny little thing to go her way? She was bone tired of everything in life feeling—and being—broken.

Suddenly the big double doors pushed open, sending the sign swinging from its twine on a single nail.

"It's fixed!" Maddie cried. "It's..."

"Hold your horses there, little lady. It's not quite fixed...yet." A tall man with messy hair and dirty hands lugged a bag of tools through the doors. The man's glance took in Maddie, then Margie, and finally raised his eyes to see Marilyn. *"Ladies,"* he corrected to the plural. "Little and—" he added a silky touch of flirtation to his tone "—not so little."

Marilyn couldn't quite place the face, but it was familiar. Wander Canyon wasn't so big that the familiarity surprised her. Growing up here, she recognized most faces around town, even after having lived in Denver since her marriage. "We were hoping to ride today," she told him, even though it felt like stating the obvious.

"Well, I was hoping to have it fixed today. As it is, I'm waiting on a part from New York. I can't exactly duck down the street to the hardware store on something like this. So no rides yet. Sorry 'bout that."

Maddie's pout filled her face and pinched Marilyn's heart. "No rides."

The man set down his bag and crouched down to Maddie's level. "Afraid not. Which is too bad, because you look like just the little girl to look perfect riding the bluebird." He turned to Margie, making a show of considering her. "And you, well, you look to me like a zebra kind of girl."

"I like the rooster best," Maddie said with great importance. The Wander Carousel was famous for sporting a full collection of unusual animals—fish, grasshoppers, lambs, birds, mice—but not a single pony among them. Every Wander child had a favorite, and they got to ride for free on their birthday. Marilyn's twins, who'd been coming here to visit since they were toddlers, were no exception. It wasn't their birthday, thank goodness, but the disappointment still stung.

The carousel mechanic's sky-blue eyes looked an

amused sort of pained, if that made any sense. "Well, what do you know. I'm usually good with picking people's favorites." Looking at Margie, he scrunched up his face in mock thought. "Am I wrong about you, too?"

"The zebra's okay," Margie said, always eager to please. "But I like the seahorse best."

He sat back on his haunches. "Wrong about both," the man said. "Seems I'm off my game."

"Guess Mom's!" Maddie said, somehow thinking this guessing game would rectify things.

"Maybe I should." The man straightened up slowly, scratching his chin in dramatic consideration as he rose. Marilyn felt as if he was giving every inch of her a once-over.

Which was how she recognized him. Just as he reached his full height—almost a head above her—she knew he was Wyatt Walker.

Wyatt had been a year or two ahead of her in high school. Too handsome and nowhere near enough well behaved, he'd been one of those boys mothers warned their daughters against. Charm and trouble wrapped up in a package that too many girls found irresistible. Not that she'd ever been one of them. They didn't travel in anywhere near the same social circles, and Marilyn doubted they'd said three words to each other in high school. But she knew who he was, because *everyone* knew who Wyatt Walker was.

If she recognized him, he didn't seem to recognize her. "Hmm," he said, still staring at her. Those mesmerizing eyes were a Wander High legend. "I'm going with...the owl."

She was relieved he'd guessed wrong. The gleam in his eyes told her he'd read too much into being right. "Actually, I've always been partial to the ostrich."

The moment she said it, the fact struck her as telling. An ostrich. The perfect choice for a woman who'd had her head in the sand for the last year and a half. *Ouch.*

He rolled his eyes and shook his head. "Wrong on all counts? I don't know quite what to do about that. Except maybe introduce myself. I'm Wyatt Walker." He pulled a bandanna from the back pocket of his jeans and wiped his hand before extending it for a shake.

Marilyn wanted to say, "I know," but instead shook his hand and said "Marilyn Sofitel. These are my daughters." She touched each of their shoulders as she named them. "Margie and Maddie."

"Hi," said Maddie, holding up her hand for a shake. Landon had always said his daughter would grow up to be president of something, given her outgoing nature.

"Hello, Miss Maddie. Nice to meet you." He gave Maddie's hand a formal shake, then held out his hand to Margie. "That makes you Miss Margie, does it?"

Margie, a bit of a tomboy, wrinkled her nose at the title. "Just Margie." Landon had touted this daughter as the one who would invent something amazing.

"Well, just Margie, my name is Wyatt. Nice to meet you. Sorry about the carousel. Are you staying for the summer? Will you be here long enough to come back when it's fixed?"

"We live here now," Maddie said. "At Gram and Gramps's house."

"Till we get settled on our own," said Margie. Marilyn gulped at how her daughter parroted the words of a recent conversation. A conversation Marilyn had had with her parents the other night when the girls were *supposed* to be in bed. She raised an eyebrow at Margie, who responded with a too-innocent *who me?* shrug.

Wyatt considered her again, thoughtfully this time. "Sofitel. Do I...know you?"

Marilyn wasn't quite sure if she should be glad or annoyed that she'd changed so much since high school. Those days felt a world away, and she certainly felt like a different woman from the cheerleader who had steered well clear of a boy like Wyatt. "Actually, we went to the same high school. I was Mari Ralton back then."

"Mari Ralton." She watched recognition light his eyes. Those bright blue eyes and sandy blond hair—rebel long back then but cut shorter now—had been his hallmark back in the day. He still was an attractive man, if one went in for the "misunderstood" type. "I think I remember you." He squinted his eyes in thought. "Cheerleader. Debate club, maybe? Not my class, though. One year behind?"

"Two, actually. I moved to Denver when I got married." She tried not to sigh. "And now we're back." She gave Wyatt a pointed look that she hoped told him she didn't want to get into *why* she was back.

He caught her meaning—sort of. "Well, then," he said to Margie, "bring your dad with you when you come back and I'll say hello to him, too. Maybe I can get *his* animal right."

Marilyn felt her chest tighten just as Margie's chin tilted down and she said, "You can't."

Wyatt offered her a questioning look, as if to say, *care to respond to that?*

"My husband passed away last September." She was still waiting for the world to stop turning for a handful of seconds every time she had to tell someone that.

It was to Wyatt's credit that he addressed his response to her daughters. "I'm mighty sorry to hear that. It's a very sad thing to lose your daddy." He raised his eyes to Marilyn. "I'm sorry for your loss. Glad your folks are here to help. Ralton—Ed and Katie, isn't it? Down on the south side of the canyon?"

That was Wander. Everyone knew everyone else. "Yes, that's them." The small-town friendliness was a good thing, mostly, only in her situation it made Marilyn feel a bit trapped. She hadn't counted on the closeness rubbing so raw here. People had been nice, but she still felt too exposed. It was an uncomfortably tight squeeze to poke back into town salvaging the pieces of a once-pretty life. The promising girl who married well and moved away only to have to crawl back home.

Stuck and broken. A bit too much like the pretty carousel that sat immobile behind those big doors.

Nice one, Wyatt. Bad enough you haven't fixed the carousel yet, now you bring up two poor little girls' dead father? Today was proving a nonstop tour of coming up short on things. Not quite sure what else to do, Wyatt offered Mari—*Marilyn*—as much of an "I'm so sorry" look as he could manage with the little girls staring straight at him.

"You still on the ranch?" Marilyn's question held a "let's please change the subject" tone. He couldn't really blame her, given the sad subject he'd raised.

Oh, if she only knew her deflecting question raised an awkward topic of its own. "Um...no."

She, of course, looked surprised. "Really?"

Wyatt shifted his weight to buy himself a scrap of time. By now he'd hoped to be done explaining why he'd moved off the family land and into the apartment above Manny's Garage. Not many people—make that almost no one—in Wander could understand why a Walker would step away from Wander Canyon Ranch like he had. Most people scowled at him as if it was a genetic fluke—or at least a phenomenal disappointment—to bear that last name and not have ranching in his blood. Reaching for what you want in life shouldn't have to feel like letting everyone else down. He tried to keep his tone conversational rather than irritated. "Chaz runs the ranch now. Or most of it, now that Dad's trying to be retired. And married."

"Oh," she said, nodding. "Mom said something about your dad's new marriage. And Chaz, too, right?"

Dad and Chaz's recent marriages had indeed been the talk of Wander's wagging tongues. It had been a relief when the Wander gossip mill focused on Dad's fast marriage to Pauline. And then his stepbrother Chaz's taking over the ranch. And then Chaz's surprising marriage to Pauline's niece, Yvonne. A little Wander Canyon soap opera tailor-made to shift the spotlight off him. The cascade of those three dramatic events had made it easy—well, *easier*—to slip out of his son-and-heir status when it came to the ranch.

Of course, it hadn't been anything close to easy. He'd wrenched himself out from under that yoke with pure brute force and open rebellion. Chaz was over it, Dad was trying to get over it, but the rest of the town hadn't been so gracious. After all, it wasn't hard to pin a new underachievement on Wander's established bad boy. He was actually surprised Marilyn didn't already know—but then again, she'd been living in Denver. Most days he sloughed the scorn off, but the sideways glances and disapproving tones were evidently getting to him. How else could he explain the sudden, uncharacteristic offer to not only help Manny out, but to step in and fix the carousel when it broke?

"The ranch was never really my thing," he admitted, using his now-standard explanation. Wyatt nudged his tool bag with one boot. "I'm covering Manny Stewart's auto shop for him for a while."

"And fixing merry-go-rounds," one of her girls added. Which one? He couldn't hope to tell the girls apart. Two sets of big brown eyes—three, if you counted their mother's—with two bouncy sets of pigtails to match. Marilyn's hair was a tumble of brunette waves, so the girls' straight hair must have come from their father. He didn't remember much about Mari, just that she was part of the popular crowd he steered well clear of. The kind of girl who got awards and good grades and stacks of teacher recommendations on her college applications.

"I'm trying," he replied. An unexpected sour spot grew in his stomach from disappointing the little girls. He still hadn't quite figured out what made him step up to play the hero and fix the famous Wander Carousel when it broke down right before Memorial Day weekend. The loyal good-guy bit was his stepbrother Chaz's thing.

It certainly wasn't turning out to be *his* thing. So far Wyatt had only found multiple ways to fail. Finicky mechanisms, obscure parts he couldn't quite figure out how to order—the carousel felt like a puzzle he couldn't quite solve. It lacked the straightforward functionality of the car engine he knew well. Every day those carousel animals stood still bugged him a little bit more.

He pulled out the small notebook he always kept in the back pocket of his jeans. "Tell you what. If you give me your phone number, I can call you to come have the first ride when it works."

Marilyn gave him a look. Ah, so she *hadn't* forgotten him. There was a time when collecting women's phone numbers had been a spectacular talent of his. Still was, if the filled pages of that little notebook were any indication. The right kind of woman always had a soft spot for the wrong kind of man.

"For the girls," he emphasized, adding his best contrite look. If she did remember him like her current scowl implied, she should know dating widowed mothers was definitely not in his wheelhouse. "For disappointing them today."

She did not look convinced, nor did she offer a phone number. He flipped the book closed and slipped it back into his pocket. "I've got another idea, then." He pulled out his wallet and produced a small red tag with his signature on the back. Holding it up, he said "Go on over there to the Wander Bakery." He pointed to the shop down the block his new sister-in-law purchased this past winter. "Give this to Ms. Yvonne inside. She'll know it means I said you could have any cupcakes you wanted. On my tab."

"Cupcakes!" the girls shouted in perfect unison. "Mom, can we?" asked one while the other tugged insistently on her mama's sleeve.

"And whatever you want, too," he added to Marilyn, handing her the ticket. "I figure it's the least I can do until I get things up and running in there."

She took the ticket with a reluctant smile. Marilyn was pretty, elegant even, with delicate features and the creamy skin of a well-to-do woman. And while that chin tilted up a bit too much for his taste, she also had a tired, scraped-thin kind of look. She held herself too erect—like someone afraid of toppling over. She forced up the corners of her mouth in a way that told him she hadn't had too many genuine reasons to smile of late. The stance of a soul just barely holding it together. Given the sad news she'd told him, it was likely true. "That's very kind of you." Her tone was overly formal.

Kind? Maybe. Mostly just opportunistic. In his experience, only the rare female turned down free baked goods. Especially ones as good as Yvonne made. Dates who'd been canceled on, disappointed garage customers, moms of customers, most anyone could be easily appeased with something from Yvonne's bakery. Running his "red ticket tab" at Yvonne's had been one of the smartest ideas he'd ever had. His new sister-in-law might give him grief over it, but it had come in handy for a whole host of reasons, business and otherwise.

"Which one do you like?" a tiny voice asked.

"Cupcakes? I go for the double chocolate," he replied. "And Yvonne makes them with a whole pile of frosting, just the way I like it."

A set of pigtails bobbed in giggles as one girl pointed to the building behind him. "No, silly, I meant the animals. In there. You tried to guess our favorites. You didn't tell us yours."

Wyatt told the truth as he flashed his most charming smile. "Me, I like 'em all."

Over the top of the girls' heads, Marilyn gave him a look that said *some things never change*. Clearly, she wasn't referring to cupcakes.

Yep, she remembered him all right.

Chapter Two

"The merry-go-round was still broken." Maddie's pout was as wide as Wander Canyon as they walked in the door of the Ralton family home.

Marilyn's mother looked up from her knitting. "You're kidding. I was sure it'd be fixed by now."

You could have told me to check, Mom. Marilyn tried to tamp down as many disappointments as possible for her girls since moving back. It took a heroic effort to paint this move as a happy, positive step, and she needed all the help she could get.

"But we got cupcakes," Margie countered, holding up the box of coffee cake Marilyn had purchased for the following morning. "For free."

Dad came in from the backyard, wiping his hands on a towel that hadn't been white since Marilyn was in high school. "Sounds like a pretty good deal to me."

"They weren't exactly free." Marilyn took the box from Margie and set it on the counter.

"The nice fix-it man got 'em for us," Margie explained, producing a "care to explain that?" look from Mom.

"We met Wyatt Walker coming out of the carousel building. The cupcakes were his idea. He runs a tab at the Wander Bakery, evidently."

Mom's scowl spoke volumes. "I don't know who thought it would be a good idea to let Wyatt Walker try to fix that carousel. I guess I shouldn't be surprised it's still not running." The carousel was a source of huge civic pride for the small town. Which made it not at all the kind of thing anyone would be quick to put Wyatt in charge of handling. Marilyn was ashamed to admit she'd had the same thought.

"He's supposed to be mechanically inclined, so maybe they thought it'd make sense," Dad said. He peered into the bakery box and sniffed. "Cinnamon. My favorite." He gave Margie a conspiratorial wink. "Should we connive to have some now?"

Margie loved "conniving" with her grandfather. Both girls had terrific relationships with their grandparents. It was the only thing that eased coming back to Wander with her tail between her legs. Of course, Mom and Dad still didn't know the half of it, and Marilyn hadn't yet decided whether or not to keep it that way. Was it easier to bear if no one knew? Or would the secrets about Landon only fester? After all, her work in public relations had taught her that some secrets—actually most secrets—never quite stay hidden the way you'd like them to. But what would ever be gained by people knowing the truth about Landon? Surely it was better if the girls' memory of their father remained the upstanding man most of Denver hailed him as.

Marilyn plucked the box from her father's grasp and set it up on top of a cabinet by the bread box. "This is for tomorrow. Little girls who had cupcakes for lunch don't need to have coffee cake, too."

"Well, *I* didn't have any cupcakes for lunch." Grandpa adopted an oversize version of Maddie's pout.

"We had peanut butter and jelly, too," Margie argued. Marilyn was glad the new young owner of the bakery Ruth used to own had offered to toss in a pair of PB&J sandwiches "on the house" to go along with Wyatt's gift of cupcakes. It kept lunch from being a total nutrition loss. She'd felt compelled to buy the coffee cake just to be nice in return.

"All in all, sounds like a pretty good afternoon for a failed carousel trip," Dad declared.

"Mr. Wyatt's gonna call Mama when it's fixed so we can get the first ride," Maddie announced.

Mom's eyebrow went up. "Is he, now? Got your phone number, did he?"

"No, he did not." When the girls looked as if this might dampen their chances for the first post-repair ride, Marilyn added, "He knows we're staying with you, so if he wants to make good on his offer, he can."

That brought an alarmed look from Maddie. "Won't he?"

Don't, Marilyn warned Mom with her eyes. *Let them just think of Wyatt as the nice man who's fixing the carousel. They don't need to know we both know he won't keep that promise.*

Dad stepped in. "Well, if he doesn't, I'll take you there myself the second I hear it's up and running. After all, it's been too long since I've been on a porcupine."

Margie's eye went wide. "I forgot about the porcupine!"

"Best carousel porcupine ever," Dad said. After a second, he shrugged and added, "Maybe the *only* carousel porcupine ever." He looked at Marilyn. "You favored the ostrich, didn't you, sweetheart?"

"Mr. Wyatt guessed wrong on all of ours," Margie pronounced. "I don't think he's very good at it, even though he said he was."

"Imagine that," Mom muttered under her breath as she finished a row and turned her work.

"Why don't you run upstairs and get your crayons so you can get started on those coloring books we bought at Redding's?" Buying a toy at the town general store after a ride on the carousel was one of the fixtures of Marilyn's childhood. It felt good to at least keep that part of their outing. And besides, it was next to the Wander Chamber of Commerce, where she'd dropped off her resume. She couldn't sit around and play grieving widow forever.

Mom set down her knitting as the girls barreled past her toward the stairs. "How'd it go with Gail?"

Gail from the Chamber of Commerce had been kind and polite, but how much staff did a small-town organization need? Marilyn couldn't honestly say if the woman had taken her resume out of genuine interest or as a favor to her mother. Did it really matter which? "She said she'd look at it and keep an ear open for possibilities."

"Sounds promising," Dad said.

"Sure," Marilyn agreed, even though she didn't.

She opted to change the subject. "So what's the story with Wyatt Walker off his family's ranch?"

"Foolish boy," Mom said, rising to put the kettle on for tea. Marilyn found Wyatt a bit long in the tooth—and long on masculine looks—to be called a boy. The way Mom said it, you'd think Wyatt had just been caught smoking outside the high school gym. Which, come to think of it, he had been. Multiple times.

"Never could quite figure out why he'd do that," Dad said. "That ranch is Hank's pride and joy."

"But Chaz runs it now, though, right?" Chaz Walker was Wyatt's stepbrother. His wife was the woman who owned the bakery now. She'd liked Yvonne instantly, even felt as if she could be friends with the woman.

Dad got a trio of mugs down from the cupboard, ignoring mom's *tsk* as he opened the coffee cake, clearly not intending to save it for tomorrow. "I'm not so sure Hank ever really got over Wyatt just walking away from Wander Canyon Ranch like that. I'm not even sure what he does now."

Marilyn got out the sugar. "He told me he's helping Manny Stewart with his garage."

"A garage?" Mom balked. "When you could have all that land?"

Not really my thing. That's how Wyatt had put it, hadn't he? Rather casual for a stunning rejection of the family estate. There was a story there. "Maybe not everyone takes to ranching."

"Maybe not everyone takes to hard work." Mom's words had sharp, judgmental edges.

A man who volunteered to fix a complicated old carousel didn't strike Marilyn as being allergic to hard work. Then again, her marriage had proved how wrong she could be about men, hadn't it?

Wyatt looked up from draining a Jeep's brake fluid to see a shapely silhouette standing in the garage bay door. Not a bad way to start a Friday. He put down the bucket and wrench he'd been holding and picked up his charm. "Well, hello there."

"Hi. My car needs an oil change." She walked into the garage and Wyatt realized that silhouette belonged to Marilyn Sofitel. "I figured showing up here was the least I could do after you bought my daughters cupcakes yesterday."

Chaz never believed that Wyatt's cupcake tab at Yvonne's was effective marketing. It was always fun to prove Chaz wrong. "Cute kids. I felt bad disappointing them." Given how long it was taking to fix the carousel, this wasn't turning out to be the easy way to score points with the town fathers he'd planned. Not that delayed parts coming from Albany was his fault, but he wasn't sure folks would see it that way. People were always quick to judge, but he'd learned to slough it off just as fast.

"Oh, to hear them talk, they came out ahead. Cupcakes go a long way with those two. But I warn you, they plan on holding you to that first ride. They talked about it all the way home."

"I'll try to make it happen soon." Yvonne had told him about Marilyn's visit with the twin girls. She'd given him a good ribbing about how taken the little girls had been with "the Carousel Man."

Wyatt had enjoyed many reputations in his day—

still did—but he wasn't quite sure he was ready to be known as "the Carousel Man." That title belonged to the slightly kooky old guy who'd built the carousel. When he'd died a month ago, a carousel committee had been formed. But when the first malfunction happened, Chaz convinced Wyatt to help. It was supposed to be a temporary thing. Stopgap Carousel Man. Certainly not Wander Canyon's new purveyor of childhood joy. Even for cuties like Maddie and Margie. Or their mother.

"So." He motioned toward the sensible upscale vehicle sitting just outside his garage. "Oil change?"

She gave the car a dubious look and produced a small notebook out of her handbag. "According to this, at least. I'm just learning how to handle stuff like this. Landon was—" she searched for the right word "—*particular* about cars." It fell just short of a compliment, a telling mixture of awkwardness and resentment.

"It's not a bad thing to learn how to be particular. I'd much rather service a car that's been well looked after than one that's been ignored." He flashed her a smile. "Although, I admit, I make more money on the ignored kind."

She laughed, but there was a tension in it. Life had really taken a couple of hard swings at this woman, hadn't it? She was prettier than he remembered her being in high school. Her glossy hair framed a delicate face with features he could describe using only the word *tender*. She moved like a woman still off balance and highly bothered by it. Wyatt wasn't quite sure what gave him such an insight. He normally didn't bother to read women that deeply. Perhaps it was the contrast of her current striving to the girls' faces of easy joy yesterday.

Being charming came to him as easily as breathing, but he was struck by the overwhelming urge to be nice to her. Genuinely, decently nice, not just the kind of nice designed to get him a phone number or a date. Huh. His upstanding do-right brother, Chaz, might have a lot to say about that, but thankfully Chaz was not standing in his garage watching him give Marilyn a kind smile.

"I'm not a lot of things, Marilyn, but I am honest." He held out his hand for the book, which he expected to be a meticulous maintenance log. "Let me look at this, and the car, and I'll help you figure out what needs doing."

"Thanks." She said the word easy enough, but just before she did, there was a flick in her gaze. A short burst of something behind her eyes that told him someone had given her plenty of reasons not to trust.

He flipped quickly through the book, confirming that it was a detailed listing of all the vehicle's maintenance and repairs. "Thorough."

She sighed. "My husband was nothing if not thorough."

Setting the book aside, Wyatt walked out to the vehicle and slid his hand under the grille to pop the hood. He could live with her suspicions, even dare himself to live them down. He did that all the time, after all. He barely even registered the sideways glances of folks in town anymore.

The SUV's hood rose to reveal a pristine engine.

"You weren't kidding." *Particular* was an understatement for the kind of care this car received. He bent down over the engine, and whistled in appreciation. "I doubt you'll have much to worry about with this car."

She glanced back at the shop. "Have you worked at Manny's long?"

He looked farther and removed a spark plug, unsurprised to find it in perfect condition. "Nah. I've just been filling in for him while his wife gets her knee fixed. I'm still trying to figure out my long-term game plan." *Now that I've booted myself off the family ranch, that is.*

"Open your own garage, maybe?"

Wyatt straightened up. "Dunno." He wasn't sure what made him test her with the next statement—her newness back in town, maybe. "Might be something for me if that new hotel keeps expanding." He watched her reaction, knowing full well her parents were one of the most vocal opponents to the project. "You know about that?"

She frowned, her face taking on the scowl most Wander residents did when discussing Mountain Vista. "Dad's been talking about it," she admitted.

The resort firm had been looking at a large-scale expansion in the area. Word had it some offers had been hinted at to a few of the less successful ranchers. As far as he knew, town disapproval had kept any of the landowners from admitting to considering an offer, but Wyatt knew it was only a matter of time.

They'd known better than to approach Dad or Chaz about ever selling Wander Canyon Ranch. Still, Wyatt's buddy Tim had started talking to him about coming on board to run the maintenance and vehicle fleet—if the expansion went through. Sure, it was an unpopular project, but it wasn't as if he had an upstanding reputation to forfeit.

He shut the hood of the vehicle. "And what's your opinion?"

She gave him just the hint of a challenge with her eyes. "I can't say I'm in favor of it myself."

So she *did* have a bit of fight left in her. He kept his words casual as he wiped his hands. "They have an uphill public relations battle ahead of them, that's for sure."

She straightened. "I work in public relations. Or did. But I prefer causes I believe in."

He pushed out a breath and motioned for them to walk back into the garage. "I believe in fast cars and good steaks. That doesn't mean I don't work on slow little Volkswagens and eat my share of chicken wings." He handed her back the maintenance logbook. "'Course, we all know being respectable's never really been high on my priority list."

"Even if I didn't care about *integrity*—" she gave the word a sharp emphasis "—I'm not really in the market for that kind of drama."

He laughed at that. "Well, you came to the wrong place to hide out from that. We may look charming from the outside, but I expect we rank as high in the drama department as whatever fancy Denver suburb you came from. Or don't you remember?"

"I loved growing up here."

Her declaration had the edge of forced hometown pride that always drove him nuts. "Good for you. Three cheers for Wander Canyon." Why was everyone always insisting Wander was so idyllic? It had never struck him that way—just the opposite, most days.

"If Wander's so bad," she challenged, "how come you never left?"

She definitely had some fight left in her. *You try getting out from underneath Old Man Walker and see how far you get.* He didn't have the luxury of some well-heeled city tycoon sweeping her out of here to go tend to some tasteful three-car garage house at the end of a quiet Denver cul-de-sac. He met her glare for a long moment before saying "Reasons," with a little more hiss than he ought to. "Look, you only need an oil change and I can do that easy. But if I don't rank high enough on the integrity scale for you, feel free to head on over to the dealership twenty miles east of here and let him charge you forty dollars more for inferior oil. It won't bother me none."

She hoisted her handbag higher up on her defiant shoulder and turned toward the door. "Well, when you put it that way…"

What was the matter with him? Picking fights with customers? Manny would kill him for starters, and he liked to think of himself as capable of more charm than that. "Wait. Stop."

She did, which surprised him.

"Look, I was out of line." He ran a hand down his face. "I'm just a little down on Wander at the moment. People are getting on me about the carousel and all. No reason to take it out on you and your tidy little ride there."

"I get it." She actually looked like she did. When

you spent lot of time at the end of your rope, it wasn't hard to see it in other people. Somehow, at that moment, he could see that Marilyn wasn't home by choice. He wasn't quite sure how he didn't see that yesterday—maybe she put up a good front for her daughters—but her eyes broadcast it now loud and clear.

He walked over to her. "I'll be glad to change the oil for you. And write up what ought to come next and when, if that'll help. Least I can do for jumping down your throat like that."

She shrugged. "It wasn't very fair of me to ask you why you hadn't left. Everybody's got reasons."

Those last three words hinted at a lot. What were hers?

Chapter Three

Marilyn stood in the middle of the sidewalk, half fuming and half stumped. Wyatt had told her to come back in an hour and a half, and Mom had taken the kids to the grocery store with her.

She now had time to herself. Taking in a deep breath, Marilyn looked up and down Main Street, surprisingly stumped as to where to go next. Wander was the kind of small town people would call quaint, with a classic Main Street lined with mom-and-pop businesses, the kind of restaurants where everyone knew your name, and was generally blessed with clear sunny days perfect for meandering. The morning ought to feel like a holiday, the peaceful, blissful stretch of time she'd often dreamed of in Denver's hustle and rush.

Now, thanks to Wyatt Walker, she couldn't quite figure out what to do with it.

The man unnerved her. How did anyone get away with not caring what anyone thought of him the way he did? In a small town like this—actually, even in a big city like Denver—that seemed impossible to her.

You couldn't indulge in that kind of disregard. Good, upstanding people *had* to care about their reputation. Community standing still meant something, didn't it? Her parents had taught her that. She was still trying to hang on to that belief. Of all the things Landon had taken from her, she wasn't going to let integrity be one of them.

Wyatt Walker declared himself "honest." She believed him to be—blatantly, even tactlessly forthright. Honest was one thing, but Wyatt was also defiant and more than a bit reckless. Truth be told, if the messy state of the garage was any indication, he was also rather disorganized. If she clung to anything in life, it was organization.

So why did she care even one whit about how messy the man kept his garage? It wasn't as if he needed efficiency to recommend his work. He had been—and clearly still was—handsome enough to get away with just about anything he wanted. She wouldn't be surprised if he had more female customers than male. After all, he wielded that dashing smile like he knew exactly the effect it had…on other women.

Well, it wasn't going to have any effect on her. Marilyn wasn't even the slightest bit interested in romantic relationships. Especially with men in possession of dashing smiles. Even if she found some perfect man here in Wander Canyon—which was unlikely at best—people might talk. Small-town vistas always looked quaint, but small-town tongues could be cruel. She guessed a year—if not more—would need to pass before any date she might go on wouldn't immediately be labeled as too soon. The fact she was such a young widow wouldn't matter.

The fact that her marriage to Landon had grown cold couldn't matter, because she couldn't let that come to light. Not even her mother knew how the love had somehow drained out of her marriage to Landon. She couldn't bear for anyone to know how powerless she was to stop Landon's growing disregard. Oh, they looked happy from the outside—Landon always made sure of that. Marital strife was unacceptable for Denver's next promising candidate for the state Senate. He'd made it quite clear that her role was to smile, look happy and tout him as promising and successful. There were days Marilyn felt she was married to a resume, not a loving father and husband. It had become a lonely way to live, and his death simply deepened the emptiness.

Nope, she told herself. None of that. The very last thing she needed on this glorious morning alone was to give in to any kind of pity party. These days had to be about looking forward, and getting herself and the girls settled.

Marilyn sat for a moment on one of the rough-hewn log benches that dotted Wander's Main Street. Taking a deep breath, she closed her eyes and fell back into the ritual that had gotten her through the months since Landon's fatal car accident. *Three things I'm glad for, Lord, and three things I need.* How many times had she stopped wherever she was and taken a moment to thank God for three little blessings in her life and ask Him for three small needs? There had been scores of dark and panicked moments since that somber-looking pair of police officers had arrived at her door. How many times had those blessings and that dose of provision pulled her back from the brink?

I'm thankful to have found an honest mechanic.

I'm thankful to have a morning to myself.

I'm thankful the girls are excited about starting school here.

I need to feel like I have a plan—or even just the start of one.

I need a job. Or maybe even just an interview.

I need a friend.

Right there was perhaps the reason Wyatt Walker had unnerved her so. He was being friendly, and she desperately needed a friend. Of course, one could never count on Wyatt's friendliness as just that. Did the man even know how to be friends with a woman? Even a definitely not-in-the-market widow with children in tow? The absurdity of that thought almost made her laugh.

A plan. This morning's solitude was exactly what she needed to get started on one. Opening her eyes, Marilyn chose her next step. Lunch and planning. She rose resolutely off the bench and began walking away from the garage and the unnerving Wyatt Walker and toward The Depot. The little railroad car diner that sat next to the carousel felt like the perfect place to ponder her next steps. A quiet lunch where she didn't have to cut the crusts off anyone's sandwich seemed as good a place to start as any.

She ordered a lovely, grown-up salad and iced tea, and reached into her handbag for the notebook she always kept with her. Marilyn had just uncapped her pen when she noticed a woman standing beside her table.

"Mari?" A vaguely familiar face popped into view. The bright-eyed, curvy woman in a brightly colored scarf peered down at her, a to-go container balanced in one hand with an enormous cup of soda in the other. "Is that you?"

Marilyn was surprised and grateful the woman's name popped up out of her memory. "Tessa?"

"It *is* you. I heard someone at church say you were back." Tessa Kennedy glanced at the empty place setting opposite Marilyn at the small table. "You all by yourself here? Want some company?"

She did. Desperately. "Oh, I don't want to keep you."

Tessa sat down immediately, as if it were no big deal. "You're not. I keep telling myself not to eat at my desk anyway."

God's little provisions. They never failed, did they?

Tessa flipped open the cardboard container to reveal a heap of deliciously rich-looking macaroni and cheese. With a generous portion of barbecued pork piled on top. The delectable smell suddenly made Marilyn's salad look far too sensible.

Tessa smirked and leaned in. "The fast-breaking news at the *Wander Gazette* really isn't that fast-breaking, if you know what I mean."

"That's right, you were a journalism major." Marilyn hadn't known Tessa that well in high school, but they'd kept up a bit over the years. She'd always been friendly, and clearly that hadn't changed.

Tessa stirred ice in her drink. Mari remembered she

drank vats of diet cola in school, and evidently that hadn't changed, either. "Yes, well, it'd be a stretch to call me a journalist now. Small-town reporter struggling my way through single parenthood of a teenage boy comes a bit closer." She paused to let Marilyn's memory catch up while she tackled the mound of food with her fork. "Nick and I split a year after Gregory was born. Mr. Right hasn't shown up yet, so it's just me." Her hand stilled and her face changed. "Oops. Me and my mouth. It's just you now with your girls—twins, isn't it?—I'm so sorry."

"Landon's been gone nine months."

"I remember reading about that accident. We ran a story on it, seeing as how you were from here and everything. He seemed like a great man and a huge loss."

She never knew how to respond to statements like that. To lots of people, Landon was a great man. For her, he'd stopped being that well before he died, and that never seemed like the kind of thing to say out loud, ever. "Yes," she replied.

"The single-mom thing. No easy road, is it? At least you've got cute little girls. Teenage boys defy explanation, let me tell you."

"The girls are a terrific comfort to me." It sounded corny and poetic, but it was true. Maddie and Margie were absolute lifelines to her right now. "A real blessing."

Tess grinned. "I try to remember that Greg's a blessing. Some days it's harder than others. Where are your girls?"

"Mom took the girls to the grocery store and shopping for school backpacks so I could bring the car in for service and have a morning to myself. They start first grade here in the fall."

"Little pink backpacks," Tess practically mewled. "They probably have sparkles and kittens on them, huh?"

"Margie's never been the pink sparkly type. Maddie will come home with something girlie, but Margie is just as likely to pick out camo."

Tessa's laugh was warm and welcoming. "Hey, I've seen pink-and-purple camo."

Marilyn thought of the bedspread from home Margie insisted come to Grandma and Grandpa's with them. "Oh, believe me, so have I."

Tessa's face lit up with a thought. "Hey, you should come to Solos. It's the single-moms Bible study at our church. Decent baked goods—Yvonne over at the bakery donates them, and that woman knows her stuff—and free babysitting. Spiritual fulfillment aside, it's the cheapest girls' night out in town. You free Tuesday evening?"

Marilyn was nothing but free. Her calendar held more open space than all of Colorado's state parks combined. "As a matter of fact I am."

"Well—" Tessa dug back into her meal "—that settles that." She lifted a heaping forkful of the incredible-smelling dish. "I'll never finish this. I *shouldn't* finish this. Want to share?"

Marilyn felt a little of the weight slide off her shoulders. "Sure."

Wyatt gripped the phone handset, ready to hurl it through the garage wall. "No, I don't want to hold, I want you to ship me the right part now and..." He fought the urge to growl as he heard the telltale click, then syrupy instrumental music echoed from the other end of the line. *Not again.*

He stared at the parts catalog page and back to the packing slip inside the box he'd just opened. Why didn't anyone use plain English for these things? Car parts, truck parts, even carousel motor parts—why use such a complicated code of letters and numbers? Why couldn't a six-inch pinion gear be a "six-inch pinion gear" instead of Part #XH770? All that nonsense made it hard to tell parts apart—and almost impossible to make sure the part you wanted was the one that showed up in the shipping box.

Case in point? The much-needed gear he'd ordered for the carousel. The one that was too small. Again.

"I just need the next size up!" he grumbled uselessly into the receiver, fully aware that the awful music meant no one was on the other end of the line to hear him.

Wyatt considered banging his head on the workbench. The road to eternal torment was surely paved with tedious paperwork. When did life become such a mountain of irritating correspondence? Dad used to say he could smooth-talk a snow sale to a penguin, but fill out an order form? Wyatt would happily live in a world where no one ever had to fill out forms.

He pulled the receiver away from his ear, scowled at it and punched the zero on the keypad half a dozen times. *Give me a human, not a phone tree.*

A decidedly inhuman voice informed him, "You have entered an incorrect selection. Please try again."

Wyatt exhaled, reminded himself that his worst day at the garage was still better than his best day on the ranch and waited. After an eternity, the oh-so-polite woman returned to the line. "I appreciate your patience, Mr. Walker."

"Can we please just fix this? Fast?"

"I'm doing my best, sir."

Wyatt hated being called sir. In his experience, no one who ever really wanted to help you called you sir. He pinched the bridge of his nose, grimly reminded that the gesture was an echo of Dad's. "And?"

"I have reviewed your account. The part you received is the one you ordered."

"No, it's not. I need the next size up, not this one."

"You ordered part number XH760. The next size up is XH770."

Wyatt peered at the packing slip, endlessly annoyed to see she was right. He tossed the offending sheet back into the box. "Whatever happened to small, medium and large?"

"You can exchange it, sir, but I can't authorize expedited shipping if the error was on your part."

"Tell that to Margie and Maddie!" Wyatt growled into the receiver.

"Tell *what* to Margie and Maddie?"

Wyatt spun around to see Marilyn Sofitel back in his doorway. He stuffed a lid on his boiling temper, pointed to the phone receiver and gave her a "hold on a second" expression.

"Fine. Expedite it. I'll eat the surcharge. On this order and the one from yesterday. Are we square?"

"Yes, sir. We appreciate your business."

Tell that to Manny. And the guy who owns the Jeep still waiting on the right air filter. *I hate this part of the job.* More than that, he hated the thought of giving Manny anything else to worry about.

Wyatt clicked off the call. "If they call it a help line, they ought to actually *help* you, don't you think?" He'd botched no less than three orders in as many weeks. Since when did car parts feel more like algebra?

"Everything okay?"

He slapped the parts catalog closed with more force than was necessary. "Not when they tell you it'll be thirty extra bucks for expedited shipping. They can't get the order right for the broken carousel part. Stupid order numbers."

He watched her eyes roam to the piles on the desk in the corner of the garage. He'd let the paperwork pile up.

"Orders not coming in on time?" she asked.

He didn't want to admit his frustrations, especially to her. "Something like that. Late or wrong. Honestly, I don't know how Manny ever could keep track of all this stuff."

Before he could stop her, she was walking toward the desk. "He must have had some kind of system."

He did, and he'd explained it to Wyatt—twice—but the disorganized pile of papers on the desk practically advertised his inability to follow it.

Marilyn, on the other hand, looked like the kind of person who alphabetized her spice rack. He stepped between her and the cluttered desk in an attempt to head her off, but she went right around him. "There's that logbook there," he called after her, pointing to a tattered blue binder sitting open on the desk. "But I don't need to use it."

That wasn't exactly true. He'd tried to use it. It just

wasn't working for him. And he sure wasn't going to drag Manny in here to explain it a third time. *I just gotta get a handle on it, that's all.*

She ran her finger down one page and got a look on her face that was 100 percent know-it-all mom. "What goes wrong?"

He hesitated, trying to come up with an answer that didn't make him feel like an idiot. Eventually, her relentless gaze and his desperation cut his pride down to size. "I keep ending up with the wrong stuff," he admitted, finding a grease spot on the garage floor to look at. "Part numbers and I...don't exactly get along."

He waited for her to laugh. Or make some nasty remark. When she didn't, he looked up to see soft, kind eyes. "Margie doesn't get along with numbers, either. She says they hate her."

"I hear her loud and clear." Shouldn't she ask his permission before moving papers around like that?

"Some people are better with their hands than with paperwork, don't you think?" She started flicking through the stack of files. "I mean, Margie's only just finished kindergarten but she can draw way better than I can." She looked up at him. "Landon used to joke I could file in my sleep."

He couldn't stop himself. "Is your spice cabinet in alphabetical order?"

Now it was her turn to look sheepish. "I know better than to rearrange my mother's spices. It's not my kitchen."

"But your kitchen? Back in Denver?"

"Organization is important. And it saves time."

Wyatt pointed at her. "So it is...well, was..."

"Maybe."

Wyatt nudged the box containing the too-small carousel pinion. "I'm wasting time I can't afford to waste with these dumb mistakes. The carousel's bad enough, but customers are getting peeved that repairs aren't done when I promised them."

"On account of parts orders coming in wrong?"

He looked over at the Jeep two days overdue because of a dashboard part. "Or not coming in at all. I was sure I ordered the part for that, but the dealer says I didn't."

Marilyn sat down at the desk. "It shouldn't be that hard to get this under control." She picked up a file. "An hour's worth of sorting sounds like a fair trade for free cupcakes."

"Those cupcakes were for the carousel. There's nothing says you have to help me."

She got that look again. Where did woman learn to pin you with their eyes like that? "Didn't your mother ever teach you to say thank you when someone offers to help?"

He hated the idea of admitting to anyone in Wander that he might need help keeping orders straight. But seeing as she was a newcomer, maybe it wouldn't be so terrible if he let her help him get things in order. For an hour.

Wyatt swallowed his pride and gulped out, "Thank you."

She smiled. "You're welcome. Will it be okay if I come back Monday and we get started then?"

"Sure thing." He had to admit, for a fancy-pants, hyperorganized city girl, she had one heart-stopper of a smile.

Chapter Four

What had he done? Wyatt flipped on the lights in the garage Monday morning with a sense of stunned surprise. He was here half an hour before the garage even formally opened—rather a shocking turn of events for someone with his night-owl tendencies. Even Yvonne at the bakery gave him a look when he came in for some doughnuts. He'd known she would, of course, and almost went to the market on the other side of town, but that felt like treachery. Yvonne had been good to him, even when he hadn't fully patched things up with Chaz.

Marilyn's arrival felt like an invasion, which made no sense. Except for the thrumming sensation that she'd see things. Things he didn't want her—or anyone, for that matter—to see. He was Wyatt Walker, the smooth guy with all the answers. Unfortunately, the mounting pile of disorganized invoices and receipts on the desk wasn't interested in keeping up appearances. He'd tried once more over the weekend to make sense of the paperwork and still came up short. The honest truth was that if Marilyn hadn't offered help, he was going to be forced to find it somewhere, and soon. With her help, he wouldn't have to turn to Chaz or Dad or Yvonne or even Pauline to sort this out, and that was a good thing.

Setting the bakery box down beside the coffeemaker, Wyatt told himself the two pink doughnuts were to thank Maddie and Margie for letting him hijack their mom for the morning. Sweeping up the garage floor yesterday afternoon was just plain common courtesy, that's all.

At 8:30 a.m. on the dot, Marilyn's car pulled into one of the parking spaces outside the garage and she pushed open the door. Her punctuality didn't surprise him one bit. Morning people baffled him. How all that energy and focus were in a man's brain so soon after waking never made sense to him, and was one of the first clues he wasn't cut out for up-at-the-crack-of-dawn ranch life. To Wyatt's way of thinking, a man was meant to ease into the day, and enjoy long nights.

"Good morning." Bright eyes welcomed him over a set of large coffees from Yvonne's. "I brought coffee."

She'd been to Yvonne's? They must have just missed each other. Wyatt could just picture the grin on his sister-in-law's face—and likely the amused text she was sending Chaz. "We have some here, but Yvonne makes it better."

"She said the same thing. She also said you'd picked up doughnuts when I tried to buy some to bring over."

Wyatt switched off the coffeemaker. "No sense organizing on an empty stomach."

Marilyn hung her coat neatly over the back of the

desk chair and checked her watch. "Mom is going to drop the girls off on her way to a committee meeting at ten thirty, so I've got two hours to make a serious dent in this." She sat down, looking unnervingly eager to tackle what he'd dreaded. *Paperwork* and *pleasant* didn't come in the same breath in his world, but she looked as if this was fun. "Where do you want to start?"

He gaped at the pile, not wanting to admit that he'd already tried to start—and failed. "I have no idea."

"Is there any order to what's on this desk?" The words could have been judgmental, but they didn't have any bite to them. Curiosity, maybe, as if she couldn't quite comprehend how messiness happened, but not the disappointed edge his father had down to an art form.

"Chronological, I suppose. Oldest on the bottom, newer on top."

She peered under one of the larger piles. "Like an archaeological dig?"

He had to laugh at that. "Yeah. Only no treasure at the bottom."

She leaned down, reaching under one of Manny's notebooks. "You're wrong there." With a triumphant grin, she held up a twenty-dollar bill and waved it at him.

"You're not going to say finders keepers, are you?"

"I promised to help, didn't I?" After a beat, she added, "Just how much do you think is in here?"

"I hope that's the last of it." He did, actually. Even though the ancient cash register made more sense to him than the evil torture device that passed for

Manny's credit card machine. That thing had it out for him, he was sure of it.

She stared at the desk for a long moment, eyes narrowing as she tucked her hair behind her ears. Hatching, he realized, a plan of attack. "Sort first, then assess."

She had a system. With stages. Wyatt swallowed hard. Out of nowhere his brain concocted a vision of Maggie and Margie dancing in a circle singing "Sort first, then assess" like it was the best game ever. "Um…meaning?"

"I make piles, then we sort each pile into smaller piles based on what needs doing first."

That didn't sound too painful. He was worried she would take one look and say she'd have to come back tomorrow with a truckload of office supplies. After all, she looked like the kind of woman who owned a label maker. Or three.

He ventured the question that worried him most. "So what do you need me to do?" Sitting opposite her on the desk having to fess up to multiple layers of disorganization ranked right up there with oral surgery or cleaning out the cattle barn.

"Oh, I don't need your help just yet. You can go ahead and do whatever work you have to while I…excavate. Once I get the piles made, though, we'll need to go through them together."

How did she not make it sound awful at all? "Okay." The gush of relief that went through him was downright invigorating, although he took pains to hide it. If "sort first, then assess" got him to the spot where Manny walked back into a smoothly functioning garage without overdue orders or lost paperwork, then he'd welcome those four words as his new favorite phrase. "I can get behind that plan."

With no hesitation or concern, Marilyn picked up the first two pieces of paper, stared at them and started making piles.

And piles. And more piles after that. In fact, after twenty minutes or so, Wyatt looked up from a tune-up to find her *humming*. As if she was enjoying watching the mountain of mess transform into a dozen or so stacks of papers. Half hiding behind the tires of the car up on the lift, Wyatt watched her consider an idea, reach down into her handbag and produce a little leather wallet thing. With a satisfied smile, Marilyn pulled out a pack of those sticky notes Chaz was forever using. She planted a note on the top layer of each pile, labeling it. For him? For her own amusement? Who knew?

Since he found himself at a good stopping point, Wyatt made a show of stretching his back. "Is it time for a coffee break yet?" He wasn't entirely sure he wanted to examine the piles she'd created, but a surprisingly large part of him wanted to let her show him. Mostly because she looked like she'd get such a kick out of it.

She pushed the chair back from the desk. "Perfect timing—I've just gotten everything sorted out."

He walked toward the desk. "You don't say." She really had done it. You could see the actual wood of the desk—something he hadn't seen in weeks—underneath the collection of tidy piles. Each with its own colored sticky note. It didn't surprise him that her handwriting was curvy and precise. What did it say about him that his own handwriting was spiky and nearly impossible to read?

Marilyn gave him a sideways glance. "You might have avoided half of this by staying on top of things in Manny's notebook. His system is simple, but pretty effective."

He knew Manny's system was simple—to Manny. The man explained it as if it were child's play, which only made Wyatt feel worse about not catching on. He simply shrugged, not wanting to admit to any kind of struggle in something she seemed to find so easy.

"It's like housework," she explained. "If you just keep up with it, everything is far easier."

Reaching for the doughnut box, Wyatt gave her a look he hoped translated to "housework comparisons don't help one bit."

"Remind me never to show you upstairs," he laughed, and then instantly regretted how inappropriate that sounded. "I live upstairs," he tried to clarify, but it only made it worse. "It's not at all neat." Finally, unable to dig himself out of that particular hole, he flipped open the box and said, "Doughnut?"

This was a different Wyatt Walker. He was missing the glint and the swagger, and was more softly spoken without the continual persuasive edge his voice had carried years earlier. She'd noticed the new bag of upscale flavored coffee next to the work-a-day tin of grounds next to the coffee machine. Was it there for her benefit?

Marilyn could far more easily imagine Wyatt peeling bills out of his wallet and whispering in some woman's ear "Get us a couple of coffees, baby" than she could see him picking out a bag of French Vanilla Hazelnut from the roasters up the street.

Even more telling was the pair of pink-frosted doughnuts doused in sprinkles. She couldn't resist. "Partial to sprinkles, are you?"

Wyatt shifted his weight and coughed. "I thought I ought to get something for the girls."

The small kindness tucked itself in her chest where the emptiness usually dwelled. "You don't have to buy froufrou coffee for me, you know."

He seemed relieved to hear it. "Yeah, I got a couple of weird looks buying it."

She'd have thought the valentine-hued doughnuts would have brought more stares. "Not used to stares?"

"Not the French vanilla kind." He winced as he drained the enormous mug he'd kept on the workbench. "Like drinking a candy bar. Don't get me wrong—I love candy. But not hot in a mug before lunch."

She wasn't sure what made her ask. "It doesn't bother you? The way people talked?" It felt kinder to put the verb in the past tense, even though Mom had made it rather clear that people still talked about him.

"Depends on who's doing the talking." He picked up a heavily frosted chocolate doughnut. "I can tune out my dad easy." After a moment he added, "Or your mom and her friends."

It shouldn't have surprised Marilyn that Mom's judgmental words eventually found their way to Wyatt's ears. Like most small towns, there were precious few places to hide from the glare of gossips. The bite of criticism is one of the things she worried about when coming home, why she'd held out in Denver until the girls were finished with kindergarten. Reputations were easier to keep up from a distance, and everyone still believed Landon to be the upstanding man her husband made sure everyone saw.

Wyatt mistook the silence of her thoughts for regret. "It don't bother me none. Your mom and those types. I knew by seventh grade that I'd never change in their eyes. So I made it a game, I suppose."

Marilyn found a napkin and plucked a sticky glazed cruller from the box. "A game?"

"A competition. How far down the spectrum of annoying and disrespectful can I get without crossing the line into illegal. I'm a master." He took a big bite of doughnut as if that proved his point.

There was the glint and swagger she'd come to associate with Wyatt. "Really?"

Wyatt pointed to his car where it sat in the parking lot, an enormous bold and brash pickup truck looming over her well-heeled SUV. "Did you know the legal limit for a truck exhaust is eighty-two decibels?"

She could guess where this was going. "I did not."

He nodded at the vehicle. "Eighty is just enough under to get away with it and still pull a few nasty looks if I gun it right."

"But not enough to get you a ticket."

"I carried a decibel meter and a copy of the ordinance in my glove box for the first month. They stopped pulling me over after that." He grinned. "But it still bugs 'em."

Troublemaker. He relished the role, even now. "You like to stir things up."

"The way I see it, some things need stirring."

And some things are better left to settle. As long as they don't fester. Or stagnate.

She'd been wondering most of the morning as she saw the pile of parts receipts and operations drawings for the merry-go-round. "So why the carousel?"

He sat on the edge of the desk. "I'm not even sure I know myself. Impulse, I suppose. Manny's idea, actually."

"Manny's?" Wyatt didn't strike her as the kind of man to do something just because someone told him to. Quite the opposite, in fact.

Wyatt shrugged his shoulders. "His idea of reforming me. Using my powers for good, and all." His gaze fell to the dark depths of his coffee. "Only it hasn't worked out that way, has it? The carousel's still broke and people are ticked at me on account of it." He gave the piles of paper a look as dark as his brew. "Wrong parts and misorders."

It really bothered him, this pile of messy papers. Oh, he'd never say it out loud, but she could see the annoyance—the frustration—in his eyes. He wanted to do a good job at this, and it was eating at him that it loomed beyond his reach. He cared far more than he ever wanted to let on. "Let's fix that. Or at least get a start on it." Marilyn sat back down in the desk chair and motioned for him to pull the second chair up beside her. She pointed to each of the piles in turn. "Receipts, completed orders, waiting orders, invoices, general mail, insurance, checks and miscellaneous."

"What? No pile for fan mail?"

She merely rolled her eyes. A career in public relations was nothing if not an exercise in wrangling egos. "Which one bugs you the least?"

He sat back in his chair. "They all bug me."

Resistance often showed itself disguised as defiance. Margie had given her plenty of experience in that realm. "Which is why I asked you which one bugs you the least."

He thought about it for a moment, then pointed to the stack of checks. "Those. Money coming in, after all."

She picked up the stack. "Not if you leave it sitting on a desk." She picked up one and waved it at him. "This one is three weeks old."

"I've been busy."

"You haven't been paying attention. Open those two binders over there and grab a pencil."

He looked shocked. "I'm gonna do this?"

"You won't learn if I do it for you."

"I'm okay with that."

She squared off at him. "I am the mother of two small girls. You can't get away with that kind of stuff with me."

He managed to look penitent. "Evidently not."

With careful patience, Marilyn showed him how Manny logged each check against the insurance claim or invoice listed in a set of binders. She watched his laborious handwriting as he recorded each check. She gently corrected him when he transposed numbers or letters, which he did several times. Each logged check then took its place in a bank pouch. Twenty minutes later, they'd reached the bottom of their coffee cups and the bottom of the stack of checks. A nice, orderly deposit slip sat filled out in the pouch with the checks, ready to take to the bank.

"Look at that," she said with a smile. "A nice fat deposit and one pile gone. Not so hard, right?"

"Sez you," he mumbled in mock displeasure. Mock, because there was no hiding his sense of accomplishment, or hers.

She took the sticky note that had said "checks" and planted it victoriously on the wall beside the desk. "Our wall of fame. All these sticky notes will be up there before you know it."

Now it was his turn to roll his eyes. At least until Marilyn's cell phone went off in her handbag.

"I'm out front with the girls," came her mother's voice. "Come get them." *Because I'm not coming in there* came through loud and clear.

"I'll be right there." Mom could be such a stick-in-the-mud when she chose to. "The girls are here," she said to Wyatt, ending the call. "I'll be right back."

She stepped outside and opened the car door. "You could have brought them in," she said to her mother as if it were no big deal—because it wasn't.

Mom's look spoke all the jabs she didn't say.

"Mr. Walker bought you doughnuts from the bakery." Marilyn made sure to catch her mother's eyes as she informed the girls. "Pink frosting and sprinkles."

Gleeful cheers and the rapid-fire unbuckling of seat belts ensued.

"Wash your hands, girls," Mom called as the girls scrambled out of the car and ran through the bay door.

Honestly, you'd think mechanics had cooties from the way she said it.

Marilyn waited until the girls' joyful greeting of Wyatt, and his happy hellos to them, died down. "Thanks for bringing them by."

"Will you be home for lunch?" Which in Mom-speak, meant "How much longer do you intend to stay in this awful place?"

"I'll be finished here in about twenty minutes. But I promised the girls a stop at the library, so if you and Dad are hungry, don't wait on us. Wyatt's doughnuts should hold the girls over until later."

"Well, all right then."

That was the response Mom gave when she was acquiescing to something she didn't much like. Such a long way from "yes," or "that's fine with me."

"See you soon, Mom." A small surge of Wyatt-worthy defiance poked up her spine. She'd felt refreshingly useful this morning. Able to make a difference—or at least lend a hand. After weeks of feeling like an imposition, a charity case, it was a pleasant change. She wasn't going to let Mom's grimace take that away.

Marilyn had decided an hour ago that she was coming back for as long as it took until the piles were processed and completed. Mom would just have to learn to live with her daughter—and maybe even her granddaughters—hanging around Manny's Garage for the time being.

Chapter Five

❧

"Great—you're here!" Tessa practically pulled Marilyn into the room Tuesday evening. The cozy sitting room served as the Solos Bible study meeting location at Wander Community Church. WCC was as picturesque as the rest of the town, a wide wood-shingled structure with an angled roof and a cupola that still housed a real bell. In the wintertime when the snow frosted the eaves, the church looked like something on a Christmas card. Now in the summer months, it had a rustic, almost log-cabin feel that kept it the center of much of the community. Sitting right in the middle of downtown at the end of Main Street, its community-hub feel was geographic as well as social.

Tessa spouted instructions as if people joined the group every day. "Margie, Maddie, the movie room is down that hallway. Follow Heidi and you can meet the rest of the kids." A bright-faced high school girl said hello and led the girls away to their own activity. Tessa leaned in. "They get popcorn and lemonade, we get coffee and—" she turned toward the goodies spread on a side table "—yum! It's tiramisu today."

"What's not to like?" Marilyn agreed. She stood still for a second and looked around the room. There were a lot of women seated in the circle of chairs. A surprising number of women, in fact.

"I know," Tessa agreed, catching her expression. "You think you're the only single parent on the planet some days, and then you come here." She quickly introduced Marilyn around the circle. No sign of Wander's gossipy or judgmental wagging tongues here. Only an arc of warm, encouraging expressions accompanying each new name. So much so that Marilyn had to wonder why it had taken her so long to find the courage to join the group. Why hadn't Mom ever suggested it? They all went to this church, after all.

"I saved you the seat next to me, but I expect next meeting you'll feel like you can sit anywhere. Right at home." She motioned toward a woman coming back into the circle of chairs. "Janice here has a girl where your girls will start in the fall, I think."

"Canyon Elementary. I'll be happy to show you the ropes over there," Janice encouraged as she handed a piece of the tiramisu to Marilyn and Tessa.

Marilyn drank in the warm welcome. Janice, and in fact every woman around the room, looked like a potential friend. How had she not realized she was this thirsty for friends? She'd been trying so hard to "buck up" and keep going that she'd relied totally on Mom and Dad for everything. But it would be lying to say their support, however loving, didn't come with its own set of pressures and expectations.

She felt no pressure here, just camaraderie. These were women who truly understood what it was like to face the challenge of raising two girls alone.

"This group is my lifeline. We all hold each other up here." Tessa gave Marilyn a friendly nudge. "And you can eat as much of the cake as you want without getting any looks from us. We need to take our indulgences where we find them, you know?" She looked down at her plate. "Honestly, a whole cake wouldn't last two minutes with Gregory in the room. I feel like I should just hand my entire paycheck over to the grocery store."

Marilyn thought of the struggle she'd had to get the girls to eat a healthy lunch yesterday after Wyatt's enormous pink doughnuts. Every child came with their own challenges, didn't they? "My girls are picky eaters, Margie especially."

"Mine, too," a tired-looking woman with a long red braid said. "If it isn't apples, rice or white bread, I'm in for a battle. And green beans? Ha! Not in a million years."

Everyone laughed, and Marilyn felt the knots in her shoulders ease up a little. The rest of the session was taken up with warm conversation, honest questions about life and faith and a generous dose of grace. Exactly what she needed. She made a mental note to be back next week, and every week after that.

As they were helping to put the folding chairs away, Marilyn caught Tessa's elbow. "Can I ask you something?"

Tessa placed her chair on the rolling rack that held them for storage and shrugged. "Sure, anything."

Marilyn slipped her chair in behind Tessa's. "It's more of a reporter question than a mom question. Is that okay?"

"I don't see why not. If I can't answer, I'll tell you so."

"Is everyone really that upset over the carousel being broken?"

Tessa straightened up. "Do you mean is everyone as upset as Wyatt Walker thinks they are?"

Marilyn felt her eyes widen.

"Your car's been there twice in five days. And you were there with it. And the girls." When Marilyn gave her a look, she added, "You haven't forgotten that Wander's always watching, have you?"

Marilyn swallowed a groan at the standard lament of every young person growing up in Wander Canyon. Nothing ever escaped notice in this town. "I suppose not." It explained at least some of Mom's resistance to her stint at the garage, but not all of it. While Mom had a high opinion of Hank Walker, that regard did not extend to his son. She'd even been a tad critical of Chaz Walker before he settled down with his new bride, Yvonne. She loved her mother, but there were days she could do without her intense scrutiny.

"Not to be nosy, but what were you doing there all that time?"

"Wyatt was really nice about helping me figure out what maintenance needs to be done on my car. In exchange, I offered to help him organize some paperwork that's piled up since Manny's been out. He looked a little snowed under."

"You always were the superorganized type. And he

wasn't. Isn't." Tessa reached for her handbag and the Bible study workbook the group was using. "So yes, there were some who didn't like the idea of him trying to step in and fix the carousel. Certainly no one thought it'd be out of commission this long."

"And that has people mad?"

"Maybe more like disappointed. Grumbles of 'What else did you expect from Wyatt Walker?' That sort of thing. Honestly, it's not as if some of the folks raising a fuss could step in and do better. I'd think it takes a mechanical mind, and they always said our carousel was one of a kind." She looked at Marilyn. "Feeling the heat, is he?"

"Tough to say. He's no stranger to Wander looking down on him, but I do think this bothers him more than he'll admit. I hadn't expected that. He's a bit different than I remember."

That brought a look from Tessa. "Not as much as you'd think. He's still trouble, Marilyn. Charming, but trouble. Watch yourself."

"Oh, I'm sure he finds me more of a nuisance than anything else. I just need a project, I suppose. And believe it or not, he's been really nice to the girls."

"All I'm saying is, watch yourself. Because you know, Wander's always watching."

"Seems like it." She was scheduled to go back to the garage tomorrow morning to tackle the next of the piles with Wyatt. She wanted to go back, wanted to feel the satisfaction of organizing things and of helping someone who had been nice to her. It didn't feel fair that such a simple gesture became far more complicated. But Wander *was* watching, and this was a town where everything was everybody's business.

"You know, one of the first piles I hoped to sort through tomorrow was a bunch of carousel parts orders. I think I might be able to help speed things up." She'd seen the beginnings of a trend that pointed to more than just complicated order systems. It was far too early to say for sure, and she had no idea how to address it with someone of Wyatt's oversize ego, but she couldn't just walk away with the job half-finished. The garage and the carousel would benefit if she could help. And, just maybe, there'd be a big benefit for Wyatt himself.

Was that worth the glare of Wander watching? Then again, what did it show the girls if she didn't at least try to help someplace where she could make a difference? Teaching the girls honor and integrity now fell solely to her. She couldn't help thinking that if Landon's darker side ever did come to light, they'd need a solid moral foundation on which to stand.

"It's just a short stint of paperwork," she dismissed to Tessa. "Two more days at the most. It's not like I have a packed calendar anyway. And who knows? I might get a free tune-up out of it."

Tessa held Marilyn's gaze. "Sometimes free isn't really free. You've seen him. You remember him. He hasn't changed. The man breaks hearts for amusement."

"Tessa, look at me. I think we can safely say my bedraggled self holds *no* interest for the likes of Wyatt Walker. He always dated the prettiest girls. These days I'm grateful just to manage a clean shirt and both shoes on."

Tessa laughed as they walked toward the room where the laughter of young children spilled out into the hallway. "Why is it mussed looks great on most men while it never looks good on any of us?"

Marilyn knew better than to make even a single remark about how a smudge of grease did somehow improve Wyatt's disarming good looks. She felt decades older, but the years hadn't diminished how handsome he was one bit. It wasn't fair.

"I'm not in the market," she declared, just for emphasis. "I'm not even in the county where the market is, for that matter. So you don't have to worry about me."

"Oh, I get it," Tessa said. "Most days the only man I want to date is Mr. Clean. But it's not just your opinion you need to worry about."

That much was true. Tonight's Bible study may have been filled with welcome, but Wander was still always watching.

Something was wrong with him.

Wednesday morning Wyatt stared at the small apartment he'd inhabited since his dramatic exit from Wander Ranch, flat-out baffled.

He'd cleaned it.

Wyatt couldn't remember the last time he'd voluntarily cleaned up his living space—he wasn't a tidy kind of guy. He was a throw-your-shirt-on-the-couch-and-deal-with-it-later kind of guy.

He pulled the door shut behind him, consoling himself that clean was a relative term. It was clean to him. He had little doubt Chaz, or Dad, or Yvonne or Pauline would be so quick to use the term. But you could see the floor and the chairs and tables had actual usable space on them, so that was clean.

It felt a small bit good, he had to admit. Being organized had its upside. But there was organized, and then there was *organized*. Throwing dirty clothes in a hamper and doing three days of dishes wasn't exactly the same thing as the paperwork that awaited him downstairs.

He'd kept staring at the piles as he worked yesterday, eyeing them as if they'd disperse themselves into chaos again before Marilyn came back if he didn't keep watch. He'd stacked the new mail and receipts in a neat pile of its own, even going so far as to grab one of Marilyn's infernal sticky notes and label it Incoming.

Wyatt walked downstairs into the garage bays, the fluorescent lights clicking and humming as they lit up for the day. This place always felt like freedom to him; grease and oil were the scents of independence, whereas the ranch reeked of duty and judgment. He loved it here.

The sight of the desk brought forth two emotions. A niggle of doubt showed itself as he considered the remaining piles. But there was also a tentative glow of satisfaction at the empty spot they'd created during Marilyn's first visit. A toehold of confidence that the administrative load of running a garage wasn't completely beyond him.

Before Marilyn, he'd always tamped down the notion of buying the garage from Manny when he called it quits. He told himself he didn't want the responsibility. But now that he'd managed to understand a piece of Manny's binder system, he didn't squash the notion. Maybe he could handle it. Even do well at it.

Of course, there were multiple piles still on the desk ready to prove him wrong. *I have a secret weapon, and her name is Marilyn,* he declared in silent defiance to the piles as he plunked the small bag of cinnamon coffee grounds he'd bought from The Depot counter last night. Margie had mentioned her mother liked cinnamon coffee. It wasn't so frilly a flavor that he couldn't indulge her this small touch. If they got through even half the piles today, she'd have earned way more than an oil change and maintenance advice, anyway.

Instead of heading straight into the radiator flushing that was first on his schedule today, Wyatt took ten minutes to sweep the bay floors. Again. *In case she brings the girls by,* he told himself.

Sure enough, at 9:30 a.m. on the dot, Marilyn's SUV pulled into the spot next to his truck. He looked up from his work just in time to see her glance over her shoulder before she came through the bay door. The gesture pricked at him like a thorn. *They got to her already.* Howie at the hardware store had made some ill-timed crack about the new lady in town hanging out in his garage, but Howie was a nosy idiot.

Wander Canyon had way too many nosy idiots, and the forced casualness of her look back confirmed it. She was just a person being nice to another person. They could heap all the bad intentions they wanted onto him—he'd earned them—but did they have to pounce on Marilyn so quickly?

Wyatt acted like he hadn't noticed. "Good morning," he called brightly.

She walked farther into the bay and halted, eyes casting about. Come on, a mere floor sweep shouldn't cause that much of a shock, should it?

"Manny always swept out on Wednesdays," he lied.

She kept that analytical look on her face. "Cinnamon," she said finally.

"And grease and radiator fluid," he teased, not ready to show any amusement that she'd noticed.

Marilyn set her handbag and some kind of workbook down at the desk before turning toward the coffeemaker. "You made cinnamon coffee."

"Margie outed you." It felt better to put it that way.

She smiled, as if the gesture meant more to her than he would have guessed. "That's sweet."

"Technically, isn't it savory? Or spicy? Or something?"

"Please tell me there aren't more doughnuts."

"Just coffee today. Fancy coffee, but just coffee. I've got a few minutes to finish up here if there's something else you can do without me."

She looked at the shelves of technical manuals that lined one wall. "Have you ever thought about putting these in chronological order?"

"Sure, why not?"

Marilyn poured herself a cup of coffee, and he watched the small smile curl up the sides of her mouth as she inhaled the aroma. He'd always had a knack for making women feel special. It never took much—most guys were foolish not to take note of what a woman liked and give it to her. Women were fascinating puzzles to him. Challenging and complicated. But like puzzles, their fascination wore off fast once you figured them out. Long-term relationships were as foreign to him as paperwork, and that was just fine.

"Done," he declared about twenty minutes later as he lowered the hood on the sedan he'd been working on and walked to the sink to wash up.

"Me, too," Marilyn offered. She smiled and ran her hands like a game show hostess down a neatly shelved collection of technical manuals. "Grab a cup. I was thinking we'd tackle the carousel paperwork first this morning."

Wyatt couldn't rightly say why the problems with parts orders for the carousel bugged him especially. Then again, he couldn't really say what made him take the job on in the first place. It was do-goody, civic and, as such, totally out of character for him, even if Manny insisted he was the best man to do it. The stack of misorders looming at him from Marilyn's pile on the desk would surely prove that anyone else in Wander could have done a better job.

"What do you think went wrong with all these?"

Well, that was a prying question, wasn't it? "Beats me. Parts numbers kept getting mixed up. They never send me what I ask for." He narrowed his eyes, remembering his last annoying conversation with the customer service agent.

"So it hasn't been working for you." She had that motherly analytical "Hmm, I see" tone in her voice. And a look in her eyes that made him feel like he was under scrutiny. As if she was in the process of peeling back secrets about him. He didn't much care for that, despite his fondness for big brown eyes.

Still, her curiosity beat Dad's disappointed glare by a mile. He hadn't expected to like having her company in the shop, even when they weren't talking. If she really could untangle why all his orders went wrong, he'd swallow her scrutiny. Provided she didn't get too analytical.

But she did get nosy. She walked him through each of the last four orders, asking odd questions. How he chose parts. How he filled out the complicated order form on the company's website. How he wrote things down—*when* he wrote things down, which wasn't often—in Manny's logbooks.

He was watching an idea formulate in her head. An idea about him, which both fascinated and annoyed him. "What do you need next?" she asked.

Wyatt sat back in his chair. "Another week and the Carousel Committee off my back."

She crossed her arms over her chest. "What *part* do you need next?"

He walked to the volumes she'd just organized, surprisingly pleased at how easy it was to pick the correct catalog from the orderly shelves. "Maybe this *is* better than piles on the bench."

A smirk and a raised eyebrow greeted his pronouncement. "Imagine that."

Rather than reach for a snappy comeback, he thumbed through the pages until he found the belts he needed to replace on the carousel's main mechanism. "These, in two different sizes."

"Is there an order form blank anywhere? A paper one?"

"I use the online one," he replied. "And I hate the thing."

Marilyn looked at the website listed on the cover of the catalog, pulled it up on Manny's computer and, in less than a minute, had a blank order form spitting out of the printer on the shelves behind them. "Let's try paper for this time. Humor me."

Wyatt found it wasn't hard at all to humor Marilyn Sofitel.

Chapter Six

Marilyn sat at the small desk in her room late that night, staring at a copy of the order form she'd filled out with Wyatt that morning. She'd been staring at it for the last thirty minutes now that the girls were in bed. Pondering what to do about what she thought she saw on the page.

Was her intuition right? She was no expert, certainly.

Still, it seemed clear enough to her based on what she knew: Wyatt Walker was likely dyslexic.

It explained a lot. Why he hated paperwork. Why organizational tasks confounded him. How easily—and successfully—he relied on charming other people into doing detail tasks for him. How machines came easily to him but words didn't. Why he couldn't see the point in Manny's rather clever logging system.

His handwriting was terrible, but that wasn't an indicator in itself. She knew lots of people with ghastly handwriting. He was a bad speller, too, but then again so was Landon. And these days a computer's spell-check could cover a host of those types of errors.

No, it was the numbers that offered the strongest clues. Mostly because he had the same challenges with them that Margie did. It took him several tries to get the parts numbers copied down correctly, and he didn't seem to be able to see the errors in the sequences when he made them. He could look at an engine and see what was wrong with it in minutes, but couldn't do the same on anything involving letters and numbers.

When she casually asked him what was the last book he'd read for pleasure, he looked like the words *reading* and *pleasure* didn't belong in the same sentence.

The more he talked about how much he hated the detailed paperwork now hoisted on his shoulders while running the garage, the more his complaints echoed Margie's about similar school tasks. The frustration. The bafflement over something that seemed so easy to everyone else.

I'm no expert, she told herself again as she ran her hands over the backward five on one of the earlier versions of the form Wyatt had tossed in the garbage with a growl. *I'm not sure I can help him.*

She'd had the same overwhelmed feeling when Margie's kindergarten teacher in Denver had gently raised a similar concern. "You don't have to be the only one to help her," the wise woman had said. "But you may be the only one who can point her toward help." The fact that Wander Canyon Community Church had a specialized dyslexic tutoring program had been a key factor in her deciding to move herself and the girls back home before they started first grade.

Wyatt wouldn't listen to her about something like this, would he? The man barely accepted her help in terms of office organization. His ego seemed far too large to make room for something like a learning disability. He'd see it as a defect. A weakness. Margie's own thinking about her abilities was just beginning to formulate. She couldn't risk his reaction tainting how Margie felt about herself just as she was getting ready to start a new school.

And yet there was the easy connection between them. A fast and startling friendship. She genuinely liked him, despite—or maybe even because of—how everyone else wrote him off as bad news.

Marilyn peered at the paper again, the conviction that she was staring at the source of his defiant personality rising up with the clarity of truth. He'd been brave enough to share his problem with her. Would she be brave enough to pose the explanation? More important, an explanation that had a solution?

Is it possible God put her in his path so that her experience with Margie gave her the eyes to see his situation?

"Mom?"

Margie's pouting face appeared in the light of her doorway. Hair mussed, pajamas in disarray, her precious stuffed yellow chick, Clara, hugged close. Marilyn swiveled in her chair and held her arms open. "What's up, sweetie?"

Margie tumbled into her lap and snuggled in tight. Marilyn gave her a moment to soften against her before kissing the top of her sweet head and asking again, "Why are you out of bed?"

Margie looked up at her with worried eyes. "The school's so big."

Wander Canyon Elementary wasn't a big school by her standards, but Marilyn supposed it must look enormous when compared with the cozy private kindergarten the girls had attended in Denver. As an introduction of sorts, she'd driven the girls by the school this afternoon, stopping to play on the playground while it was empty for the summer. The girls had acted excited this afternoon. Or was it just Maddie's excitement overshadowing Margie's hidden worries?

She brushed the hair out of Margie's eyes. "Big can be fun, too. But it can feel scary at first. And you won't be alone. Maddie will be there with you."

"I know." But her tone spoke that Maddie's presence might be part of her worries. New social situations came easily to Maddie. School came easily to Maddie. It didn't take much to guess that Margie was worried she wouldn't measure up to her sister.

"There are so many ways to be smart in this world. Did you know that?"

Margie didn't answer, just settled her head on Marilyn's shoulder.

"Maddie's good at numbers, but who's good at puzzles?"

She gently poked Margie's nose until she giggled just a bit and said, "Me."

"And Grandma can make great waffles, but who knows what to do in the garden?"

"Gramps."

She tightened her arms around the child. "God makes us each different. Our job is to figure out what He's made us good at and do it."

"It's not numbers, and that's what school is, isn't it?"

Marilyn couldn't escape how powerfully her daughter's words echoed Wyatt's frustration. Margie's challenges had been identified early, and she was already learning ways to address them.

Based on what she'd seen, Marilyn doubted the same could be said for Wyatt. What would years of such things going unrecognized—or worse yet, treated as a lack of intellect—do to a man's soul?

The answer came loud and clear. It would make him defiant. An outlier. A rebel. *A Wyatt.*

"Life is made up of so much more than numbers and letters. You're going to discover all kinds of wonderful things at that school. And it might be scary at first—" she angled her face until she could catch Margie's gaze "—but I promise you that in no time at all it will feel fun and exciting."

"Promise?"

Marilyn had chosen Wander Canyon Elementary especially for the strength of their specialized learning programs for kids like Margie. Backed up by extra tutoring at the church, her daughter would be given everything she needed to succeed. "Promise."

A thought occurred to Margie, and she straightened in Marilyn's lap. "Is the merry-go-round a puzzle?"

She didn't quite follow the child's thinking. "I don't know. How so?"

"Fixing it. It'd be like a puzzle, wouldn't it?"

"I suppose so."

"Well, then I hope Mr. Wyatt is good at puzzles. I want to ride the rooster."

Marilyn thought about the intensity that came over Wyatt's eyes when he stared at an engine. She saw just metal and tubes and gears, but she could see how he saw the whole mechanism and how it worked together. "I think he is. Cars are like big puzzles, so why not carousels?" After a pause, she dared to add, "Do you know I think Mr. Wyatt thinks numbers fight him just like you do?"

It was funny—and rather telling—that Margie described her inability to grasp letter and number concepts as their fighting her. It certainly fit the way Wyatt looked at the order forms and logs. The man appeared to be locked in battle.

Margie didn't seem to think this possible. "But he's a grown-up."

"There are lots of grown-ups who have the same fights with letters and numbers you do. It hasn't stopped any of them, and it won't stop you, either." In fact, she knew the physical education teacher at Wander Canyon Elementary was dyslexic. She'd hoped to find several other adults and older children to serve as models and mentors for Margie.

"So it didn't stop him?"

The question caught Marilyn up short. It probably had stopped Wyatt in more ways than he knew. More ways than it ought to. In that moment, she knew the next conversation she'd need to have with Wyatt Walker.

She'd just have to pray that the charming mechanic wouldn't put up as much of a fight as Margie's numbers.

* * *

Some days Wyatt wasn't sure why he ever said yes to these dinners.

Actually, he did know. Turns out Dad's new wife, Pauline, could be as stubborn as his father. He could turn down a hundred invitations, and she'd never stop asking. They'd been married for six months, and every single Thursday she found a reason to ask him for dinner.

Most weeks he found reasons to be elsewhere. Every once in a while he'd cave in and accept, hoping to gain a good meal and sideswipe the digs and jabs that inevitably came with it. Tonight had been long and tiresome.

He kept his eyes on the potatoes while Dad droned on about some pesky detail about the herd. Wyatt actually liked the Scottish Highland cattle they raised. The unusual breed had been one of his best ideas. One of the few implemented, in fact. He'd always been proud of that.

But it stopped there. He wasn't a rancher, and never had been. Why did Dad think pounding him with ranch details would somehow change that? Chaz was doing a great job of running Wander Canyon Ranch. It didn't bother Wyatt at all that the ranch didn't need him. He liked it that way. He preferred it that way.

Only Dad still couldn't quite see it. In fact, Dad and Chaz had spent the whole dinner talking about new tactics in vaccination schedules as if the whole thing was fascinating. It wasn't. Not to him.

"Don't you think, Wyatt?"

Wyatt did what he always did. He gave Dad a look

and said, "You already know I have no opinion on the subject."

Dad's response was what it always was: what Wyatt had come to call The Supremely Disappointed Exhale. Honestly, if there was one sound that summed up his relationship with his father, it was the sound of Hank Walker pushing out a breath while he glared at Wyatt with that edge in his eyes. He should be immune by now, should have built up a resistance worthy of a bovine vaccine, but there was always just enough of an edge in that look to cut a bit. Over and over.

And people wondered why he moved off the ranch?

"Any luck with the carousel?" Pauline asked in an attempt to keep the peace.

It was the last thing he wanted to discuss. "Not yet."

Dad cut into his pork chop. "Been three weeks."

Wyatt put down his fork. "I'm well aware, Dad."

Yvonne rose to his defense. "It's one of a kind. It's not as if there's a manual you can consult or anything, is there?"

"No," Wyatt agreed, leveling a look at Dad. "There isn't. And all the parts have to come from Albany." *In the wrong size,* he added silently.

"A motor's a motor, isn't it?" Dad scoffed.

"I don't know, Dad, is it?" Wyatt shot back, unable to help himself from rising to Dad's bait. "Are cows cows?"

Cattle was the more correct term, of course, but Wyatt was never above using the word *cow* just because it bothered his father.

"How is Manny?" Pauline cut in loudly, changing the subject. "Peggy healing up well?"

"She's having some trouble," Wyatt offered. "I think he'll be out for a while longer." That was convenient, as it gave him a ready excuse to keep his apartment above the garage and sidestep the issue of his ever moving back onto the ranch. Dad hadn't asked yet, but he would.

He didn't yet know the answer to what came next for him, even though he knew both Dad and Chaz were bothered by his lack of a plan. He'd never been one to need firm plans like they did. Like the ranch required. No amount of explaining had ever been able to make them understand how the ranch held no interest, no passion for him. Chaz had come to a baffled acceptance, but Dad still looked at him as if it was some sort of defect.

"So," Yvonne offered, clearly fishing for a safer topic of conversation. "You've got a nice young woman helping you with Manny's bookkeeping?"

Safer topic indeed. Was there some way he could fake a garage emergency right about now?

Dad looked up from his meal. "What? Who?"

"Mari Ralton," Chaz added. "Well, it's Marilyn something else now."

Surprise arched Dad's bushy gray eyebrows. "Ed and Katie's girl is helping you with bookkeeping?" He made it sound like the most unlikely thing ever to happen in Wander Canyon.

"I helped her figure out a maintenance schedule for her car now that her husband passed away. She's returning the favor by helping me handle all the annoying paperwork piling up at the garage." That was true, mostly.

"She has the most adorable twin daughters," Yvonne said with a grin. "They called Wyatt 'the Carousel Man.'"

Chaz's snort of laughter made Wyatt want to kick his stepbrother in the shins under the table like he did when they were kids. "How do they know you?" Chaz asked.

"I gave them red tickets when the carousel was broken and they couldn't ride."

Dad rolled his eyes. He'd always hated the red tickets, saying they were a cheap copout. "You better get that fixed up soon, son, or you'll be buying cupcakes for every kid in the county."

"I'm working on it, Dad." Why did everyone assume he was slacking on that job? Why didn't anyone realize it was the parts delays that were making repairs take so long?

"How come Marilyn is helping you?" Pauline asked.

"Because she's nice," Wyatt shot back, thinking it a better reply than "Because I need it."

"Because she's pretty, maybe?" Chaz teased. "You always could talk anyone into anything. I remember the time…"

"Can we not go there?" Wyatt cut Chaz off.

Pauline actually giggled. "Good story?"

Chaz nodded. Yvonne raised an eyebrow. Dad smirked and whispered, "Tell you later," to Pauline.

And they wonder why I left? Wyatt grumbled silently as he ground his teeth. Why on earth would someone as smart as Mari come back to the Canyon if she had any kind of choice?

He remembered the struggling look in her eyes, the

way she seemed to plaster a sheen of happiness on the surface in the hopes that nobody saw any of that pain whirling around underneath. Maybe she didn't have any kind of choice.

"Nothing sadder than a young widow," Pauline said with a sigh.

That look came over Dad's face again. "If you're blessed, you find love again." He picked up Pauline's hand and kissed the back of her palm. He was happy for Dad, he really was, but sometimes the new mushy version was a bit hard to take. He was worse than Chaz, and that was saying something. These dinners surely made this confirmed bachelor feel like a fifth wheel.

"You don't suppose…" Chaz didn't finish the sentence, but simply smirked at Wyatt with his hand over his heart.

Wyatt threw down his napkin. "She's a widow with two kids," he declared as if that settled everything. Because it did. He didn't think he had a type, but if he did, a single mom of twins was as far from it as humanly possible.

Chaz turned toward Dad. "I grew up in a blended family, and it turned out okay…eventually."

That was it. To call the wild tangle that had been this family over the past two years okay was the understatement of the year. "Can we *please* not go there?" Wyatt nearly shouted. He pushed back from the table. "I think I have somewhere to be."

"But I brought chocolate cake," Yvonne said.

Wyatt really liked Yvonne's chocolate cake. Still, there wasn't a cake in the whole world good enough to keep him at this table for another minute. "I'll buy myself a whole cake on Monday."

"When you pick up those cupcakes for Maddie and Margie?"

Wyatt winced. He'd asked Yvonne to make up a pair of pink-and-purple-frosted cupcakes to give the girls to keep them occupied because they were coming with Marilyn while she helped him with the last of the paperwork Monday. Now he'd never live this down. Nothing anyone ever did stayed private in this tiny, nosy little town. *Wander's always watching.*

One thing had just become crystal clear: he'd better start figuring out his future before he became the Carousel Man for good.

Chapter Seven

Late Friday morning Wyatt dumped a huge dose of cream into his coffee at The Depot. He was muttering to himself when the pastor walked up next to him.

"Tough day at the merry-go-round?" Pastor Newton joked.

Wyatt snapped the to-go lid onto his coffee, not necessarily in a rush to head back to the still-broken mechanism next door. "You could say that."

The pastor nodded toward an open booth in the train-car-turned-coffee-shop. "Got a minute?"

"Me?" Never one to hang out at Wander Community Church, Wyatt nevertheless liked the congregation's pastor. He'd always found Newton down-to-earth, surprisingly funny and devoid of the gossipy nature too many of the town's residents had. The pastor treated him as a neighbor—which he was—without regard to his church attendance or lack thereof.

Dad and Pauline, on the other hand, never missed an opportunity to remind him that he was the only Walker not to regularly fill a pew. Wyatt still believed in God, it was just church—or rather the attitudes of some churchgoers—that kept his faith on a private scale.

Wyatt's obvious balk brought a laugh from the reverend. "Yeah, you."

Even though he wasn't keen on being suddenly singled out by the good pastor, Wyatt opted to give the man the benefit of the doubt. "Maybe a break's not such a bad idea." He gestured toward the window that overlooked the entrance to the carousel building. "That thing over there's driving me nuts."

"Seems to me," Newton said as he slid into one side of the booth with his own coffee, "folks have been pretty quick to be annoyed it isn't fixed yet and in no hurry to thank you for trying."

That's *exactly* how Wyatt felt. No one else was lining up to tinker with the finicky old machine, but loads of people were ready to complain how slow he'd been to get it up and running. "Um…yeah." Where was this conversation heading? "So…?"

"So I just wanted to make sure I said thanks for trying."

No one had ever bothered to say that. In fact, most people treated his offer to help as if it were long overdue. *Wyatt Walker finally acts like a Walker. The rebel son far overdrawn on his account of community service finally pays up.*

"I have to ask. Why did you? Offer to try to fix it, I mean. No offense, but volunteering isn't exactly your style."

Even Wyatt had no solid reason why he'd stepped up when he did. "Distraction, I suppose."

"Seems to me you've had quite the talent for finding distractions. Why this one now?"

"Come on, Rev. You know things haven't been so smooth between Dad and me lately. Oh, he'll tell you it's resolved. Even Chaz will tell you it all worked out in the end. And I suppose it has." Wyatt sat back in the booth. "Settled doesn't always mean *settled*, you know?"

"You don't think your father has forgiven you for not wanting to take over the ranch?"

"Let's just say I'm learning forgiveness isn't the same thing as not being disappointed. Then again, I've made a career out of disappointing Dad, so it's hard to see why this one gets special attention." He'd already said way more than he planned to admit. Did pastors have some sort of secret method to getting things out of people like this?

"Your dad would be proud of you if you fixed the carousel."

Wyatt took a large swig of coffee to hide how close to home that statement struck. "Well, I haven't fixed it yet, so we're still firmly in Camp Disappointment at the moment." Maybe that was the reason his father's impatience irked him more than all the other complaints the Carousel Committee was lobbing his way. "It's a carnival ride, for crying out loud. Lives aren't hanging in the balance."

Newton nodded. "Sometimes people turn a little thing into a big thing for reasons even they don't understand. Still, I'm impressed you decided to give the good-deed thing a try."

Wyatt gazed over toward the Out of Order sign that

felt like it was hanging around his neck instead of on the building door. "It's not working out so good so far."

The pastor gave a small laugh. "Everybody knows no good deed goes unpunished." When Wyatt gave him an incredulous look, he said, "Believe it or not, I do hear my fair share of grousing in my job."

Right there was the thing Wyatt most liked about Bob Newton. He never pretended to be anything but human. He'd never thought about it, but pastors had to have bad or trying days just like everybody else. Maybe, given the expectations he'd barely glimpsed in his temporary stint as the Carousel Man, more than everybody else. "Huh," Wyatt replied, not quite sure how to respond.

"Don't get me wrong, I love my job. Most days. But church—like the rest of the world—is populated by humans. And humans, well, they tend to get it wrong. A lot."

Being one of those people accused of getting it wrong *a lot*, Wyatt definitely didn't know how to respond to that. He opted for his usual diversionary tactic, a wisecrack. "Hey, if it were a perfect world, you'd be out of a job."

The pastor took the crack in stride. "Good point. But it's also why I try not to miss an opportunity to say a word of encouragement when someone gets it right. Or is at least trying to." With a hint of a smile, he added, "Even if they don't show up in church often."

"Or ever," Wyatt felt compelled to amend. In fact, the last two times he'd been in a church weren't even in Wander. It was in Matrimony Valley for Dad's wedding, and again for Chaz's to Yvonne.

"I prefer to say hardly ever so far. I mean, I have to keep trying. It's in the pastor handbook."

"Oh, don't worry. Dad, Pauline, Chaz and Yvonne keep trying." He thought he owed Newton at least a shred of explanation. "Look, I'm just not a Sunday-morning-church kind of guy. God is real to me. He's just way more real to me in a clear mountain sky than in any hymnbook or stale old prayer." He realized those were rather sharp words, and added, "No offense. I'm sure your prayers are as fresh as Yvonne's doughnuts."

Newton laughed. "Now there's a compliment I've never received before. From someone who would have no way of knowing, even. Speaking of which, the other reason I came over was to pass along a high compliment someone paid you the other day." Wyatt raised an eyebrow. People weren't in the habit of paying him compliments. Well, outside of women on dates, that is. He fielded plenty of praise then.

Newton pulled a paper from his pocket, opening it up on the table to reveal a brightly colored children's drawing. *Mr. Wyatt* was scrawled in unsteady hand on the top, the *r* and *y* both backward, as were two letters in the signature "Margie" on the bottom. What the spelling and handwriting lacked, the artwork had in spades. The sheer adorableness of it tightened his throat, and he took another drink of coffee to cover the reaction.

"Margie started in our school prep program last week," the pastor went on. "In fact, Marilyn enrolled Margie in our dyslexic kids tutoring program the day after she moved back."

That was some kind of reading thing, wasn't it? Mixed-up letters and such? "Nice drawing," he said as Newton slid the paper toward him across the table. It was, actually. Not that he was any kind of judge, but it seemed well done for someone of her age. The man in the drawing actually looked a bit like him, not just some stick figure standing next to the garage's tow truck.

"She went on and on about you in the child care program when Marilyn was at church for the Solos single parent Bible study," Newton continued. "You made quite an impression. And, well, she might have said one or two things that let me know fixing the carousel hadn't been the easiest of jobs."

Wyatt gulped, wondering what inappropriate slip-ups he'd made in front of the girls. Clearly he needed more precautions than the lines of yellow tape he'd laid down on the garage floor to guide them where it was okay for them to stand and walk.

"Relax," the pastor replied to his expression. "Kids are keen observers, that's all. I mostly read between the lines. And figured someone ought to come and say thanks for all the time you're putting in to fix that thing."

Wyatt couldn't deny it was good to hear. No one had made any show of gratitude for the dozens of hours he'd spent in that red barn trying to coax those vintage gears back to operation. If anyone did talk to him about the carousel, it never strayed beyond some form of "When are you going to have it fixed?"

"Much appreciated," Wyatt managed to sputter out, genuinely surprised. "I do hate that it's not running yet, you know. No one seems to believe that."

"I expect you do," Newton agreed. "Margie and Maddie told me you promised them the first ride when you did get it to work. That's a nice thing to do to a newcomer to town. Anyone who makes a child feel special is a good guy in my book."

Wyatt managed a laugh. "Well, now, I've been called a lot of things in my day. But I gotta say, *good guy* is hardly ever one of them."

"Everybody's gotta start somewhere." He expected Newton to circle back to how good guys should go to church, but he didn't. He just smiled toward the drawing. "You keep that. Put it on your fridge or your office wall and look at it when the gripes get a bit much. That kind of thing always works for me."

Wyatt remembered Yvonne saying something about how one wall in the pastor's office was filled with children's drawings. She'd left paper and crayons out in the bakery and often posted pictures up, as well.

The pastor finished his coffee and stood. "Well, it's been a good talk. I'll let you get back to it, Carousel Man."

For the first time, the unwanted title didn't stick in Wyatt's craw. Instead, Wyatt just stared at the man in the drawing and picked a spot on the shop refrigerator to hang it up. Any defense against the growing complaints was worth a shot.

Marilyn sat in her bedroom late Sunday evening and stared at the box of photos. She'd put the task off all weekend, dreading it. She tried to spend a little time each weekend downsizing their things from the large Denver house. Whatever home they settled on next wouldn't be nearly as large. The furniture had been easy to pare down, and Dad had helped her move the pieces she wanted to keep into storage while they lived here.

It was the mementos, the huge mound of photos and keepsakes and souvenirs, that posed the biggest challenge. So much grief and regret came washing back up anytime she tried to sort through them. She'd made a long list of small steps, tackling the overwhelming project in tiny bites. It drove her crazy that it wasn't yet done, but she couldn't seem to make herself accomplish it any faster. It cost too much to hold and view these things. She had to space it out or it would swallow her whole.

Late at night seemed the worst time to do such a thing, and yet she couldn't bear to do it in front of the girls. She was, after all, preparing their memories of their father. She had purchased three boxes: one for Margie, one for Maddie and one for her. Of course they had videos—Landon had loved to take videos, and his cell phone and computer were full of them— but there was something so potent about touching a photo, holding a little trinket from a state park, or the postcard from a vacation spot. She wanted to fill these boxes and give the girls wonderful, vivid memories. Her own had become so muddied and complex that filling these boxes, painful as it was, had become nearly an obsession.

Since they'd gone to the carousel for birthday rides every year since the girls were born, that seemed like the happiest place to start.

The first birthday photo showed a chubby baby girl

on each of their laps as they sat in the hippopotamus chair. Mom or Dad must have taken the photo. *We look so happy. All that hope and promise.* The bittersweet lump in her throat was difficult, but not unbearable. In fact, the image looked so far from what her final months with Landon had been like that it was almost like looking at some other family. Landon looked affectionate and attentive. That, as much as the time stamp and the girls' young age, dated the photograph.

As a sort of painful visual experiment, Marilyn laid out the six years of photographs in a timeline. She knew what she might see, but it stung to have her suspicions verified. Even there, on their daughters' special day, Landon's wandering attention was on full display. By the third photo he wasn't looking into their happy faces. By the fifth photo he wasn't even looking in their direction. The photograph showed her face watching how his gaze was directed elsewhere. *Does my face look like that all the time? Do my daughters see that weary resignation every day?* The answer drove her to tears.

It took twenty minutes to find a pair of photographs from recent years where Landon was looking at one or both of his daughters. And despite searching through the entire collection, she could find only one of Landon looking at her. Some newspaper articles showed a carefully crafted family image—beautifully dressed wife, shiny-cheeked girls in pigtails and matching outfits— but she saw only coldness in Landon's eyes. If his hand was on her waist, it was only to turn her in a certain direction. If he whispered to her, it was to instruct, not compliment.

Was it really that bad? Was grief just tilting her viewpoint to see things that weren't there? Drumming up evidence for the shameful lack of loss she felt? Justifying the inexcusable numbness that wore the edges off her newly widowed days?

The lids made a soft *whoosh*, an exhaling sound, as they slid onto the boxes. The girls had photos of their birthdays, and their father was in each photo. That would never happen again, so these couldn't be anything but precious. *Promise me, Lord, that they won't see what I see,* Marilyn prayed as she slid the trio of boxes up onto the top shelf of her closet next to the other box, her very private locked box, the box no one would ever see.

Promise me they'll just see happy birthdays. Happy memories. Little girls should never doubt that their daddies love them.

Wives, on the other hand, could have a whole universe of doubt about husbands.

Chapter Eight

W<small>yatt</small> smiled to himself Monday morning. *Victory!*
The three orders he'd placed—or more precisely the three car parts orders that Marilyn had helped him place—arrived. *Correct.*

Finally, something went his way in running the garage. The package from Albany was due in later today, as well. If that gear for the carousel motor came in right, he'd declare it an all-out triumph. It might just be the part to get it going. How good it would feel to pull that lever and watch the carousel slowly whirl to life. To make the call inviting Margie and Maddie to have their first ride on their chosen animals. Maybe even Marilyn, too. For that matter, he'd even join in on the celebratory ride—Mr. Carousel atop an eagle of victory.

"Well, look at you!" A familiar voice pulled him from the happy vision. "What's got you grinning?"

Wyatt walked over to clasp Manny's bony shoulder. "I could say the same thing about you." Manny was, in fact, wearing the closest thing to a smile Wyatt had seen from him in weeks. "Peggy doing better?"

"Some and sort of." It was Manny's peculiar phrase that roughly translated to "about what I expected." He leaned in. "I think she's faking it. Well, partly."

Wyatt raised in eyebrow. Peggy Stewart was a no-nonsense sort of woman who'd put up with a lot over the years. *Faking it* wasn't in her vocabulary. "Oh, I doubt that."

Manny shrugged. "I worry she's getting used to having me home."

Manny was well past the age many men retired. It wasn't a stretch to think that Peggy enjoyed not having to share him with the garage. "Well, hey, is that so bad?"

"Some and sort of." He looked around the place. "I worry about here."

"No need." Wyatt gestured to the impressive piles neatly organized on the desk. The whole garage felt—and looked—more orderly than it had ever been since he'd been in charge. "Look around. I got it covered, old man." A surge of pride rose up through him to be able to say it and mean it. To be able to set Manny's mind at ease. Forget cupcakes and coffee, he'd owe Marilyn a whole cake for this moment. "Mike's picking his truck up today." He didn't hold back his proud grin. "A whole day earlier than we promised."

Manny looked so pleased. And relieved. "Oh, don't let 'em get used to that."

"Your helpers are here!" came the cry of two small voices behind them.

Manny turned to see Margie and Maddie, complete with pink and purple backpacks, trotting into the garage bay. Wyatt watched them carefully stay within the yellow tape he'd set down the other day so that the girls stayed safely away from all the machinery of the shop.

Manny scratched his chin as he took it all in: the girls, their pronouncement, the tape and finally their mother walking in behind them. "Well, now that might just explain everything." With a mischievous smirk, he added, "Sort of."

"I'm Maddie." Wyatt watched the girl extend the same confident handshake she had to him on the day they first met.

"Hello, Maddie," Manny replied, shaking hands. "I'm Manny."

"Mr. Stewart to you," Marilyn amended.

"Manny's fine, really." The old man turned to Margie. "So who are you?"

"Margie." No explanation or embellishment. That was Margie. Peggy would like her, Wyatt thought.

"Marilyn Sofitel," Marilyn offered before Wyatt could remember his manners and make an introduction.

Manny shook her hand. "Marilyn, Margie, Maddie and Manny. We're a bunch of Ms, the lot of us."

"'Cept for Mr. Wyatt," Maddie said.

"I've always liked to stand out," Wyatt said.

The girls walked over to the table Wyatt had cleared for them on their first visit, settling in as if they owned the place.

"You been hiring staff while I've been gone?" Manny made a face. "How'll they reach the hose on the air compressor?"

Wyatt was just trying to figure out the simplest way to explain this oddball arrangement when Marilyn stepped in. "Wyatt helped me figure out the maintenance record my late husband left with our car, and in exchange I'm giving him a hand with the paperwork."

Wyatt tucked one hand in his pocket. "Never really been my thing." Now that was an understatement. *Nemesis* was more accurate.

"Don't I know it," Manny agreed. He turned to Marilyn. "You got the touch. Place looks neater than when I left it."

"We get paid in doughnuts," Maddie explained. "Mom gets fancy coffee."

Marilyn's cheeks flushed at her daughter's honesty.

"Not a bad setup, if you ask me," Manny said. He walked over to the desk and scooped up the stack of envelopes sitting in a small wire rack. "Figured the electric bill's due about now, and some other things." He made a show of slowly gazing around the shop again, with the formality of an official inspection. "Seems I got nothing to worry about here."

"Not a thing," Wyatt boasted, although it might have been more accurate to say "some and sort of." Three—and maybe four—correct orders didn't quite constitute a fully running business. But it was close enough to make him happy. And to reassure Manny.

Manny bounced his gaze back and forth between Wyatt and Marilyn, eyes twinkling in amusement. "Guess I'm done here, then."

His tone made Marilyn's cheeks turn further pink. She did this thing, biting just one corner of her lip, when she was nervous or worried, and he watched her do it just then. Different from the way she pursed her lips when she concentrated or figured something out.

He shot Manny an "enough of that" look. "Peggy's missing you, I'm sure."

That made the old man laugh. "Betcha she is." He wagged a finger at Wyatt. "I'll talk to you later."

"Bye, Manny!" Maddie and Margie shouted as they waved from their spot at the table.

Manny waved as well, then headed out the door with a head shake and a chuckle that let Wyatt know he most certainly would hear from the old man soon.

Wyatt watched him leave. "Feels good to be able to set his mind at ease," he admitted as he headed for the coffeepot. He produced an actual mug this time for Marilyn. He snatched one of the nicer ones from the ranch house kitchen at dinner the other night, remembering the way she had wrinkled her nose a bit at the clunky old paper cups that normally passed for coffee service at Manny's. The girls, of course, squealed in delight at the enormous cupcakes—complete with sprinkles—Yvonne had made.

"They're huge," Marilyn cried in nutritional protest.

"Go big or go home, I always say."

One hand shot to Marilyn's hip in a very maternal fashion. "Girls, you can have half now, but I want you to save the other half for when Tessa takes you to the store."

That was a mom for you. Always taking something great like a huge cupcake and making you save half for later. He wanted to protest as much as the girls did, proving he was definitely not cut out to ever be a parent. But he also knew where his jurisdiction ended, so he kept silent as she cut the cupcakes into sensible halves. She even found a pair of plastic forks and napkins somewhere in a desk drawer to help the girls navigate all that frosting without a crazy mess. Weren't cupcakes supposed to be huge and messy?

A crazy curl of disappointment unwound in his chest at the thought of Tessa taking the girls somewhere else. Until just that moment, he hadn't realized he was looking forward to having the girls in the shop all morning. Which made no sense because he was sure he'd hardly get anything done while keeping an eye out for their safety and occupation.

And there was an equally daunting hint of tension at the thought of being alone with Marilyn. Wyatt didn't know what to do with the irrational pull that was starting to show up when he thought about her. Or sat next to her.

They worked their way through no fewer than four of the remaining piles before Tessa Kennedy from the newspaper office knocked on the garage door to fetch the girls. At that point, Wyatt found he was glad for the girls' departure. Something had clearly been bugging Marilyn all morning, and he aimed to find out what it was. She was nervous or anxious or something that hadn't been there any of the other times she'd been in the shop.

"You okay?" he asked once the girls' voices had faded down the block in the direction of Redding's general store and whatever errand they had there.

"Fine," she said quickly.

He didn't argue, but gave her a doubtful look and sat back in his chair. In his experience, "fine" meant a hundred different things to a woman, and not one of them was fine.

She responded by taking a deep breath and pulling a set of papers from her handbag. "Do you ever remember visiting a reading specialist in school?"

That was an odd question. "I remember visiting the principal's office a lot of times."

She spread the papers cautiously on the desk. "Ever remember taking a test like this?"

She looked scared. "What are you getting at?"

"It's just that... I think I might know why all these orders give you such trouble."

A spot in his gut turned cold and hard. "'Cause they're stupid and complicated, that's why."

"I don't think so. Wyatt, I think you might be dyslexic."

Marilyn watched Wyatt's eyes narrow at the pronouncement she'd just made.

"I'm not sure..." she went on. "I mean, I'm not an expert or anything. But I know enough from the treatment Margie gets to..."

Why, after rehearsing so many careful ways to say this, had she used that word? His spine stiffened. "You're saying I need some kind of treatment? Like I'm sick?"

"No. Not sick. It's a learning disability. Lots of people have it. It mixes up how they see letters and numbers."

He pushed sharply back from the desk. "I hate paperwork. That's all that's *wrong* with me." He gave the word a caustic emphasis. Then he stood up and walked away from her.

She'd expected him to bristle, to resist, but not quite

this hard. Some foolish part of her even hoped he'd welcome the theory, feel the relief of an explanation the way she had when someone had told her about Margie. Then again, even Margie had put up a fight about special class until she began to see how the skills she learned there made things easier. Why expect any less from a man of Wyatt's temperament?

"I want to help." The explanation sounded feeble, intrusive even, as if she'd poked her nose in where it didn't belong. Had she?

Wyatt scoffed. "So you were just analyzing me the other day? Seeing if your theory about my defect was right?"

"No. Not at all." She started to say more, then realized it wouldn't do much good. He wouldn't hear whatever explanation she tried to give. At least not now.

Wyatt didn't respond. He turned away from her again, slamming tools from his workbench loudly into drawers in the tall open tool chest the girls said looked like a giant red treasure chest.

He hadn't told her to leave. At least not yet. Marilyn held on to that as a good sign. "Don't you want a solution?"

"I don't have a problem."

He had a wrench in his hand, and the way his reach stilled in the air on the way to the toolbox told her even he knew that statement couldn't hold up. The desk in front of her, still piled with stacks of paperwork, made that loud and clear.

She borrowed a phrase from Margie's reading tutor. "No, you have a challenge. And you don't strike me as the kind of man to back down from a challenge."

That turned him toward her, wrench pointing in accusation. "Don't you use that parental stuff on me. This isn't any of your business."

He was right. "No, it's not. But I've always believed it's wrong not to help someone when you can."

A dark laugh erupted from him as he tossed the wrench into the drawer, the shrill metallic clatter filling the room. "Oh, yeah, you've helped." He'd always been very good at sarcasm. She'd never liked it in Landon, and it hit a nerve in her now.

Marilyn felt her hackles rise. She *had* helped. She hadn't just imagined the relief and satisfaction on his face as they'd finally begun to get ahead of the pile of papers. The way he'd talked about the orders that had come in correctly today told her everything about how frustrated he had been before. Maybe somehow to him her theory pulled the rug out from that victory, made it hers instead of his. "I think I have helped," she said gently. "I've been glad to."

She had. It surprised her how much. The time spent putting order into this chaotic space had fed her soul somehow. It was so refreshing to feel useful, to contribute something, even in such a tiny way. Sometimes the days with her parents felt like one big debt, a slippery surface of constant *not-enough* that wouldn't let her get her feet underneath her. A pressure that wouldn't let her feel strong enough to move on. That didn't make much sense, but what about grief ever did? It wasn't a logical process.

After a long, prickly silence, Wyatt leaned back against the workbench, arms crossed over his chest, defiance searing in his eyes. "And what do you *suggest*?"

She willed herself not to rise to the bait in his sarcastic tone. She pulled out the small stack of pages she'd printed out last night. Just some basic information such as a list of issues or difficulties faced by adults with undiagnosed dyslexia. She hoped Wyatt would see himself in the information the same way she saw him in there. It explained so much. To her it offered a clear hope, but she doubted Wyatt could see it that way. At least not just yet, if ever. She held the papers up toward him. "That you look at this."

"Oh, that's rich," he said with another dark laugh.

"What?"

"You tell me I have a reading disability and then you give me something to *read* about it?"

She cringed. He had her there. This had all seemed so much simpler last night. Now it just felt like a giant tangle. "You want me to read it to you?"

"No," he snapped almost instantly.

"Would you like to me to tell you what it says?"

"No."

Honestly, if he stomped his foot, she'd be hard-pressed to say if she was squaring off against a first-grader or a full-grown man.

"I'll just leave it for you, then." The poignancy of placing the printouts on top of one of the stacks of sorted papers didn't escape her. "Whether or not you look at it is up to you."

After another long pause, he said what they both were thinking. "So now what?"

"I think that's up to you, mostly." She nodded toward the stacks on the desk. "We're not done with these."

She waited for him to say something like "Oh, yes we are," but he didn't. He turned from her and walked over to the front of the bay, his tall frame silhouetted against the clear Colorado sunlight coming through the rather grimy windows. He put his hands on the huge doors and simply leaned against them, defiant and weary at the same time. As if he, who always had a witty comeback for everything, didn't have one for this.

Even as she looked at him, she couldn't fathom why the cluttered, dirty garage had felt so comfortable to a woman with her taste for order. It baffled her the way letters and numbers baffled him. Marilyn pushed away the unsettling notion that it was the man, not the space, who'd been the comfort. No. That was just her loneliness and dislocation talking, and not a voice there was any wisdom to heeding. As he stood there, not responding but not telling her to leave either, Marilyn sent up a quick prayer. *I just tried to help, Lord. I can't think You didn't have me see that for no reason. Don't let his pride get in the way of getting what he might need.*

The silence dragged on, feeding her fear that she'd just destroyed whatever surprising friendship they had. Had she let her urge to feel useful push her a step too far, meddle where she didn't belong? Landon's words, hurled at her in irritation one night when she'd been at a committee meeting for a local charity and the girls had been fighting the flu, came up from the depth of her memory. *"You don't have to help everyone. Nobody needs you like that."*

Landon had been tired and overwhelmed by the girls' sudden sickness. Caretaking had never been his strength. He'd meant that no committee needed to come before their family, but it hadn't come out that way. The bite of his words had told her *no one wants your help*. In a million little ways, Landon had made her feel that all her value came from him. As if she was an appendage, an accessory, even a means to an end. Landon had somehow worn down her self-esteem in ways she was only now beginning to realize. Maybe that's why coming home and starting over had felt like such an enormous uphill climb. Why the contents of their Denver house felt more like deadweights than treasures.

It had felt so satisfying to offer real, useful help to Wyatt. That's what had driven her to push the boundaries to help even more. It wasn't another version of Wander always watching—although it was clear that's how he viewed it.

"You probably have places to be." His voice was low, his words clipped short.

Even though Wyatt's words weren't "go home," they sent the message loud and clear. He spoke them with an undeniable finality.

Marilyn straightened the piles one last time before she left.

Chapter Nine

Wyatt slid himself out from underneath his friend Tim's derelict Jeep the next evening. "One of these days I'm gonna have to start charging you for this."

Tim handed him a battered towel. "No, you won't."

Sitting upright, Wyatt stared at the towel, then wiped his face with the front of his T-shirt instead. "And why is that?"

"I'm the only one who still plays basketball with you." Tim extended a hand to help Wyatt up off the mechanic's dolly that had sat in Tim's driveway. "All your other friends are tired of losing to you. You need me."

Wyatt merely grunted as he put his tools back in the toolbox beside the Jeep. "No, *you* need *me*. This pile of scrap would cost you a fortune if you took it to anyone else. So don't. Ever." Keeping Tim's twenty-year-old Jeep up and running was a never-ending job, but it also ensured multiple repair visits that came with the side benefits of hoops and burgers.

The visits had also started to boast an additional

feature: job recruitment. Tonight while Wyatt made repairs, Tim kept up an ongoing description of the outstanding possibilities and income potential for anyone at Mountain Vista. Honestly, Tim made it sound as if a job with the resort would solve every problem Wyatt ever had. Since Tim was looking pretty successful these days, maybe he had a point. Sure, people weren't that fond of the company and their plans to double in size, but it wasn't as if lack of public approval had ever stopped him before.

Tim ran an affectionate hand down the rusty fender. "I could never take her anywhere else."

He scooped up the basketball as they walked toward Tim's deck for the grilling portion of the evening. "So, have you thought about it?"

Evidently Tim was not going to let up until Wyatt officially threw his hat in the ring as the vehicle manager for Mountain Vista Resort. And Tim made it sound that easy, too. As if the job was his if he wanted it.

He just wasn't sure he wanted it. "I'm thinking about it," Wyatt replied to his friend. "And it does sound like a great job." Wyatt overstated his enthusiasm just to quiet Tim. "A little too good to be true" might come closer to the mark. Why would a company that big be so eager to hire someone like him?

"The pay's amazing," Tim added. "And a lot of snazzy resort benefits. The parent company has seven resorts around the country and you can stay at any of them for a fraction of what other people pay."

Tim worked at Mountain Vista as one of the resort's grounds managers. As such, Tim was involved in plans for both the current landscaping and the multiple new golf courses the resort hoped to add—three if not more. That, and two more lodging units, were behind the company's not-so-quiet attempts to buy up local land around the existing company property.

Attempts that were angering many Wander Canyon residents. Wyatt suspected one of the reasons Mountain Vista paid so well was the social cost of working for them. A connection with Mountain Vista tended to shrink a guy's friend base in Wander Canyon. Two of their mutual friends had given Tim the cold shoulder since he signed on with Mountain Vista. So although he'd never come out and say it, Wyatt guessed that lately Tim needed Wyatt's friendship as much as Wyatt needed Tim's.

"I'd have to work with you," he said to Tim. "Don't you think we'd get sick of each other?"

"It's going to be serious money," Tim offered as they walked through the house. "The company's got deep pockets. C'mon. You're over a decade out of high school. Aren't you tired of scraping by?"

"If those pockets are so deep, why you don't own a better car?" Wyatt countered. He never tired of teasing Tim about his irrational devotion to the old Jeep.

Tim smiled. "Just bought one."

Wyatt stopped in his tracks. "What?"

"I take delivery on a Range Rover next week." The look on Tim's face told Wyatt his friend had been waiting all night to deliver that shocker.

"You're ditching the Jeep?" Wyatt could hardly believe it. As a matter of fact, he found himself a bit put out that his friend had made an automotive decision like that without asking his advice.

"Of course not." Tim lit the grill with a boastful smirk. "I'll simply be a two-car guy. And when my lease is up next month, I'll be looking for a bigger place. After all, I'll need a two-car garage. I've arrived, my friend."

"Well." Wyatt leaned back against the deck rail. "Now I'll definitely be charging you. And you can't afford me."

"Don't be so sure. Like I said, the company's got deep pockets." His face lost its teasing expression. "Get on board, man. Now. I'm telling you, this is your ticket."

Wyatt ran one hand through his hair. "Me? Working for a corporation? Come on, can you really see that?"

"You'd be running your own garage, essentially."

"Yeah, of golf carts."

Tim laughed. "Well, okay, there's some of that, but only some. You'd be handling all the resort's maintenance vehicles, mostly. Think about it—your own garage, but only one customer."

That certainly had advantages. "Less paperwork," he said almost to himself, remembering the standoff with Marilyn yesterday. Anything with less paperwork had to be a good thing.

Tim winced. "Yeah, well, not exactly. It is a corporation, after all. I've done more paperwork in a month at Mountain Vista than in a whole year at my old landscaping business, actually."

He caught Wyatt's reaction. "Pay's worth it," he

added. "Totally. Come on board now, while I can pull you in easily, and you'll be sitting pretty in no time."

It was getting hard to keep stalling on Tim's offer. He was running out of reasons not to, except that something felt funny. The high salaries and easy hiring gave him a weird red-flag feeling. And then there was the trouble of leaving Manny in a lurch, which he would never do.

"So how much grief are you getting for it?" he asked, even though he knew the answer. "Toting a Mountain Vista business card?" Tim had proudly displayed the cards identifying him as "Grounds Manager" when he first got them.

Tim only gave Wyatt a dismissive look. "Some. But since when has that ever worried you?"

"Doesn't." For some reason his memory brought up the icy look Marilyn's mother had given him the day she dropped off the twins. Since when was someone like Katie Ralton worth one scrap of his regard?

"They're gonna win," Tim said. "They're already here. It's only a question of how big they grow."

That much Wyatt already knew. He'd told Dad as much. Dad's operation was too big to worry about the expansion touching him, but there were plenty of struggling smaller ranches over by Mountain Vista that would get eaten up. Maybe not right away, but soon enough. Was the smart move getting in on the ground floor like Tim had done?

It struck him at that moment, as the sizzle of the burgers hitting the grill filled the air. Tim was the last. All of his high school buddies had established themselves in careers. As in professional trajectories that were better than jobs.

And he still had a job. A job he loved, but just a job, nonetheless.

So why didn't he just extend his hand right this moment and sign on for the golden opportunity Tim kept dangling in front of him?

Wyatt hated the answer that came to him. It wasn't fear. It wasn't reputation or status or even ambition.

He was spooked by one word: *paperwork*.

"Pleeeeeease?"

Marilyn looked in her rearview mirror Wednesday morning at the pair of pleading faces in the backseat of her car. There were days every mother of young children was sure there was no weapon on earth as lethal as a persistent kindergartener's whine. *Times two*, she moaned to herself.

They were pleading to go visit Mr. Wyatt at the garage.

Dropping by the garage to visit Wyatt was the last thing she wanted to do today. Not after the last visit. The girls, thankfully, had no idea it had ended the way it had. They were oblivious to the tension between her and Wyatt. To them, he was still the Carousel Man who let them sit in his fascinating garage and bought them cupcakes. As such, she was having little success explaining why it wasn't such a good idea to bring Wyatt the special drawings they had made at Solos last night. Even though they were adorable.

"I told you, we can mail them," she persisted, smiling at the girls. "Wouldn't that be special for Mr. Wyatt to receive a great big envelope from you?"

Her suggestion was received with dual pouts. "No," Margie said in the tiny-but-oh-so-matter-of-fact voice she often wielded.

"We're going into town anyway. Why can't we visit?" Maddie made it sound like the best idea ever. Which it most certainly was not.

There was no hope for it. She was going to have to admit what had happened. Marilyn pulled over to the side of the road and turned around to face the girls. "Mr. Wyatt and I had...sort of an argument."

Maddie's eyes widened. "You fought with Mr. Wyatt?" It was almost amusing how impossible she found the idea. As if no one, ever, could find reason to lock horns with Wyatt. That was the blessing—and the struggle—of a child's viewpoint. They saw the best in everyone.

"We didn't have a fight. We had a disagreement." *A great big disagreement.*

Maddie folded her hands in her lap as if she had all of life's answers. "So, you gotta go fix it. That's what you always tell us."

And right there was another challenge of parenthood— a mother's advice could come around to haunt her. "You gotta go fix it" was often the pronouncement she made when the girls bickered with each other.

"You can use our bench," Margie offered. The time-out bench—intentionally big enough for two—had traveled with them to the new house, and was where she sent the girls to work out their petty squabbles.

The hysterical picture of her squeezed onto the tiny

bench with a scowling Wyatt next to her almost made her laugh. "That's very kind of you, Margie, but I'm not sure that's a good idea." This was a lot more complicated than "I saw it first" or "She won't take turns." Somehow "I meddled and Wyatt's denying his problem" didn't translate to the simplicities of a stint on a time-out bench.

Margie held up her drawing. She was gifted in that respect, even at her age. She could already draw things better than most adults. "Our drawings'll help. Don'tcha think?"

She had always tried to teach the girls to help whenever and wherever they felt they could. Now they were offering their little gifts in service to her, sure everything could be solved that simply. What would it say if she refused? After all, it couldn't make things any worse, could it?

"I suppose we'll have to find out."

"Yay!" came the cheers from the backseat.

Marilyn turned the corner toward Manny's garage, saying a guilty prayer that Wyatt's truck wouldn't be parked out front. But, of course, it was. "We can't stay long, though." *Please, Lord, don't let this end badly.* The girls' enthusiasm as they piled out of the car tugged at Marilyn's heart.

"Mr. Wyatt! Mr. Wyatt!" the girls called as Margie rushed to pull open the door. They piled up against each other in a halt just inside the threshold. "Where's our yellow line?"

Marilyn looked in to see that Wyatt had, in fact, pulled up the tape that showed the girls the safe place to walk. That said everything, didn't it?

Wyatt came walking up holding an open shipping box and an unreadable expression. A wrong order? A correct one? She almost held her breath for not knowing which way this would go.

"Hi," she said before he spoke, hoping the hint of pleading in her voice would say everything from *this wasn't my idea* to *let's just get through this as quickly as we can.*

Maddie took charge. "Where'd our lines go?"

Wyatt set down the box. "I didn't think you were coming back."

"Why'd you think that?" Margie balked. "We're your helpers."

Wyatt shot Marilyn a look over the girls' heads, clearly looking for a hint as to how she wanted to play this. *I have no idea,* she thought.

"We know you and Mom had a fight," Maddie declared with entirely too much ease.

"But we made these drawings for you, so we're here." Margie held out her drawing. "It's you. Fixing the carousel." She had, in fact, drawn a charming scene of a smiling Wyatt standing beside the carousel as it went around. Complete with her and her sister riding their favorite animals.

"I just drew you with a cow," Maddie said, holding out her drawing. Her cow was the classic black-and-white heifer variety, not the unique, longhaired Scottish Highland cattle the Wander Canyon Ranch was famous for, but it was adorable nonetheless.

Wyatt, to his credit, hunched down and accepted the artwork with true appreciation. "These are amazing. I love 'em. And Pastor Newton gave me the one you made earlier. Now we've got to find someplace special to hang all three."

"Where'd you put the one I gave Pastor?" Margie asked.

"On my fridge, of course." Wyatt pivoted back to squint at the small square fridge that sat next to the coffeepot.

Something in Marilyn's heart pinched at the sight of Wyatt hanging her daughter's artwork on his refrigerator. He was so sweet to the girls. He genuinely liked them, and they knew it. Had her meddling put an end to all that? Or could they find a way around this?

"Gram puts ours on the fridge, too," Margie boasted. It was true; the refrigerator at home was covered top to bottom with the girls' drawings.

"But that little fridge is way too small to hold all three. These two will have to go upstairs on the fridge in the kitchen where I live."

Maddie looked up in astonishment. "You live here?"

"Well, not here in the garage." How they hadn't broached this topic before, Marilyn couldn't say. Actually, yes she could. They'd steered very deliberately away from any talk of Wyatt's personal life. "I live in the apartment upstairs."

"Can we see?" Margie asked, craning her neck up as if she could see through the garage bay roof.

Marilyn winced. This was beyond awkward, but at least it wasn't an argument.

"Nah, not today," Wyatt said with a smirk. "It's super messy." His gaze lifted to Marilyn for a second. "And you know your mom…"

Both girls laughed while Marilyn counted the reasons why this visit had been a bad idea. She was glad Margie and Maddie seemed oblivious to the tension between her and Wyatt. If only the adult version of "go fix it" was as easy as they thought.

Margie pointed to the drawing Wyatt held. "So, is it fixed?"

Marilyn sucked in a cringing breath, and it was an awkward moment before Wyatt replied, "My argument with your mom?"

"No, silly, the carousel."

"Not yet," Wyatt admitted. He straightened up and pointed to the box he'd set on the counter. "But this part came in yesterday. Correct and on time. So maybe soon." He looked at Marilyn, but she still couldn't read his expression. Gratitude or defiance?

"So we *did* help," Maddie asserted with pint-sized glee.

Marilyn waited to see what he would say to that.

"Well." Wyatt stuffed his hands in his pockets. "How could two adorable assistants like you *not* help?" *A very clever evasion,* Marilyn thought. If he felt the correct arrival of the parts they'd ordered together was any proof of his having dyslexia, he wasn't admitting anything. At least not today.

"We're still gonna get the first ride when it's fixed, right?" Margie had no idea the weight of her question. Marilyn dared to hold Wyatt's gaze, silently pleading for him not to take their conflict out on the girls.

His eyes locked with hers for a moment, challenge sharpening his expression. Would he keep the girls out of this? Or would he penalize them for what Marilyn was sure he considered her meddling?

Wyatt squatted back down to Margie and Maddie's level. "Now, do I look like the kind of guy to go back on a promise like that?"

Marilyn's heart loosened in relief as the girls replied in unison, "No, sir."

He playfully poked each of their noses, bringing forth peals of giggles. "That first ride is yours, guaranteed."

That high note seemed like the perfect place to make an exit. "Time to go, girls. I'm sure Mr. Wyatt has lots to do today. And so do we."

Wyatt watched Marilyn put the girls into their booster seats in the backseat of the car. His reaction to the surprise visit stumped him. He'd hated pulling the yellow tape up off the floor. It left him with an aching sensation in his chest that returned when the twins tumbled into his shop. He liked having them here. And that was as far from a classic Wyatt response as you could get.

He was sorry he'd squared off against Marilyn. Oh, he still resented her intrusion, her know-it-all declaration of his problem. The doubts that had crept up over the Mountain Vista job, however, wouldn't settle. The persistent, annoying, unwelcome notion that she might be right was chasing him like a hungry dog.

He couldn't escape the fact that the first three orders to come in right in weeks had been the ones she'd helped him make. The latest one was sitting there on the counter, brazenly correct, staring at him from inside a mound of packing peanuts. The fact that it was the carousel part just seemed to make the whole thing harder to ignore.

He didn't want to let her leave now without saying something, but what on earth was there to say? He wasn't ready to admit anything to her, didn't want her to stay and poke her nose further into his life, but at the same time he felt irritated and sour about her leaving. When she closed the girls' car door, Wyatt felt his breath hitch, knowing she'd climb in the front and drive off in a matter of seconds.

He didn't know where to file the sensation he felt when Marilyn hesitated with her hand on the door handle, then turned back toward the garage and walked inside.

"Thank you," she said. Her voice had a lost, doubtful tone that pushed on his chest.

"For what?" he asked, even though he knew why.

She tilted her head in the direction of the car behind her. "For not letting them know how ticked off you are at me."

He had been ticked off at her, at first. Since last night, as the cloud of Tim's offer had hovered over his mood and his sleep, his doubts had diluted. Now they were a moat of wary defensiveness that made it hard to know how to answer her. "It's nothing." That felt far from the truth on a bunch of levels.

"I'm glad your orders came in right."

"They did." He expected her to claim that as some kind of victory, or justification, but she didn't. Wyatt glanced over at the desk, where two piles of papers still sat. Now there was also a new stack of mail and receipts growing next to the old piles. It had been so calming, so easy to work through the papers with Marilyn, that he'd avoided tackling any new paperwork without her.

He couldn't believe what he was about to do, but it was as if the question escaped out of him before he could stop it. "So, you...um... You want to come finish?" He stuffed both hands in his pockets, practically cringing from the lack of confidence in his voice. Why did this woman and her girls pull the rug out from underneath him like this? He threw a quick glance in the direction of the desk. "Those, I mean."

Two words that Wyatt never uttered were *help me.* Still, there was no denying the request hidden in his words. It made his whole body—perhaps his whole soul—itch to say them.

It seemed like an hour before a small smile crept across her face and she said, "How about Saturday?"

He didn't know if he'd admit to anything about her theory. He didn't know if he'd read the papers she left. He didn't even know if they'd end up in another argument Saturday morning. He just knew that reaching into his tool drawer to hold up the roll of yellow tape gave her all the answer she needed.

Chapter Ten

As they sat having coffee at Yvonne's bakery Friday morning, Wyatt decided to take the risk of testing Chaz's view on a Walker working at Mountain Vista.

He got exactly the response he predicted. "You can't be serious." His stepbrother's face darkened almost immediately at the suggestion Wyatt was even considering the offer.

Wyatt stirred his coffee, glad he'd opted to have this conversation off the ranch. "Well, I get they're not exactly popular."

"As in, everyone hates them," Chaz pronounced. "They're gobbling up Wander's smaller ranches. We're trying to fight it and you want to sign on to help? Seriously?"

"Wander's smaller ranches are failing. Or on the brink of failing. If Mountain Vista doesn't buy them, they'll end up as housing developments. At least as golf courses they stay open spaces."

"A golf course hardly counts as a consolation prize." Chaz scowled as he ate another of the oatmeal raisin cookies that had always been his favorite. A sensible contrast to Wyatt's sweet tooth. "I can't believe you're actually considering this."

"It's a really good offer. Not everyone is doing as well as you and Dad."

It was a poor choice of words, and Wyatt could just see Chaz biting back a comment about how the only reason Wyatt wasn't doing as well was because he'd chosen to walk away from Wander Canyon Ranch.

I'd rather be broke on my own terms, he reminded himself. Some nights, when he couldn't sleep, Wyatt would pick at that old familial wound. He was Hank Walker's biological child. Chaz had been adopted through Dad's second marriage after Wyatt's mother had died. He'd always found his lack of talent and passion for ranch management to be a cruel joke. The sour irony was that the stepbrother sitting across the table from him was ten times the Walker he'd ever be, no matter what blood ran through his veins.

There was a time when people thought of Chaz as the more sullen Walker brother. Not anymore. Chaz was so happy and settled now it made Wyatt's teeth hurt worse than Yvonne's sweetest fudge.

"You can't go work for them," Chaz pressed.

"Says who?" Wyatt named the generous figure Tim had laid out for him the other night, satisfied at how it raised Chaz's eyebrows. "That's serious money, and I'm not exactly getting rich at Manny's."

The "if you'd only come back to the ranch" hung silently in the air between them, the way it always did. Chaz had the decency not to say the words—a grace Dad didn't always possess. He'd had to fight so hard to break free of his father's absurd notion that the blood son needed to inherit Wander Canyon Ranch. Chaz and he had actually come to blows over it the day he finally told Chaz he didn't want the ranch.

While he and Chaz had made a tenuous peace over things, it still felt impossible to go back. And Chaz was doing a great job of it anyway. His father might still balk at the idea that Wyatt had never been the man for the job, but Wyatt had always known. The one thing in that whole mess he could be proud of was that he'd been honest to himself.

"So now that they're dangling all that money in front of you, why haven't you said yes?"

This was the conversation he'd wanted to have with Chaz. "My gut. I'm seeing a few red flags."

"Like…"

"Like why me? So fast and easy? Come on, even I know I don't have the kind of résumé that should generate an offer like that."

Chaz ate another cookie. "What does Tim tell you?"

"He says they want to hire local. Some very brochure-sounding language about keeping roots in the canyon. Community, that sort of thing."

Chaz gave a grunt. "Community would be going someplace where you don't have to buy up land that's been in families for centuries just to make the eighteenth hole." He leaned his elbows on the table. "A big salary won't impress a woman if it's from a company the whole town hates."

Wyatt sat back. "Who says this is about impressing a woman?"

"When *isn't* something with you about a woman?"

Yvonne had the poor timing to walk up to the table and hear her husband's accusation. "A woman with adorable twin daughters, maybe?"

"Marilyn?" Wyatt made sure he looked shocked.

"She's been at the garage a bunch. You're buying pink and purple doughnuts. Margie made you a drawing at the church learning center. And rumor has it the first working carousel ride has been promised to a pair of young ladies."

"What is it with this town?" Wyatt raised his voice. He put on the most sensible, serious face he could manage. "Marilyn is helping me organize the garage paperwork."

"Is that something like Heidi Daniels helping you with algebra?" Chaz adopted the most annoying smirk. "Because I recall that helping somehow involved kisses on the steps behind the library and..."

"No!" Wyatt shouted. "I am not hung up on Mari Sofitel. Not even close." He rose from the table. "I just may take that job for the sheer fact that it might tick you all off enough to never talk to me again." He threw a twenty-dollar bill down on the table. "This one's on me. I'm not so keen on you thinking you owe me anything at the moment."

Wyatt pushed the door open, not caring that it nearly snapped on its hinges from the force of his annoyance.

Marilyn and the girls had just finished up lunch when she pulled open the door to see Tessa and Gregory. Mom and Dad were at a Carousel Committee meeting, and Tessa had called and asked to come over.

That was a bit odd in itself, but the fact that she'd brought Greg along just made it odder.

Tessa's voice was tight. "I asked Greg to come along and play with the girls while we talked. Okay by you?"

Marilyn felt a prick of panic rise at the serious look in Tessa's eyes. Why did Tessa need to speak to her alone? "If you can push a swing, you'll be a hit." She heard the girls come down the stairs behind her and turned to make introductions. "Maddie and Margie, you've seen Greg in church, haven't you?"

Greg offered a wave. "Hi." The boy's greeting was far from enthusiastic. He'd clearly been pressed into distraction service here, which rose a cold lump in Marilyn's stomach.

Tessa leaned down to Maggie. "Your mom tells me you've got a new swing set?"

"Just last week. In the yard." Margie pointed to the back door. "Wanna swing with us?"

Greg looked like he'd prefer to be doing anything else, but Tessa nudged him in the direction of the backyard. "Sounds like fun, right, Greg?"

"Uh...sure," Greg said, shuffling behind the girls, who raced toward the swings oblivious to his reluctance.

The minute the door closed, Tessa produced a large manila envelope out of her handbag. "Greg's not the best babysitter on the planet, but we need to talk out of the girls' earshot and this can't wait."

"Want some coffee?" Marilyn asked, unsure how to play hostess to the way Tessa was acting.

"No." Tessa's usual friendly, bubbly nature seemed nowhere in sight.

Marilyn felt her pulse raise. She'd just begun to believe that she could leave the strain of Denver behind her, but whom was she kidding? Tessa's expression broadcast bad news. Marilyn forced a question out from behind the knot building in her throat. "Tessa, what's up?"

Tessa's took a quick glance out the windows to see Greg dutifully pushing the girls on the swings. "I'm not quite sure how to do this."

It was then that she knew. Maybe she'd actually known all along—or at least guessed—but it was so tempting to believe that Landon's secrets wouldn't follow her here and push their way to the surface. She'd found files in Landon's desk the week before he died. Schemes. Backroom deals. Things just short of illegal. She'd always known she'd only seen the smallest part of it, but like the ostrich, she'd buried her head in the sand.

Marilyn attempted a deep breath—really more of a gulp of a prayer for help—and sat down at the kitchen table, motioning for Tessa to do the same. "You're not quite sure how to do what?"

Landon had always made it easy to be the ostrich. He was very good at hiding things, at crafting appearances, at telling her his business dealings weren't ever anything she need to bother about. Part of her could guess whatever it was Tessa was about to show her, while another part of her realized it could be anything—even things far worse than what she already knew.

Tessa opened the envelope. "I don't know if it's better to hope you already knew this, or that you don't. Either way, I figured I owed it to you to see it first."

Marilyn's throat tightened. "Know what?" She felt a spinning, falling sensation. This was no wondrous carousel dizziness. This was a stomach-lurching drop off a cliff.

"The Denver paper's been sniffing around Mountain Vista for a while. They've wanted to do a story on the conflict between commercial and ranch land. You know, tourism corporations encroaching on natural resources, big company versus the small family ranch, that sort of thing."

That issue wasn't new to Marilyn. Most Colorado residents took sides regarding land use. She chose her response carefully. "Landon had talked about things like that when he eyed a run for the Senate."

In public, Landon had positioned himself as a supporter of the small family ranch, of protection for open lands and natural resources. Even though his legal practice focused on finance and accounting cases, he was crafting a carefully constructed public persona. In the months before his death, she'd come to suspect his public positions weren't his true values. In fact, she knew he was courting the deep pockets of resort companies in preparation for a campaign. They'd been on a few lavish vacations she guessed to have been gifts. Weekends at resorts she didn't think they could afford, always with an "order anything you like" invitation even though she never saw the bill.

When she questioned him, he'd always brush it off as if it was a necessary task instead of an enticement. "This is how we play along," he'd said. "It's the cost of gaining leverage." Only he never said leverage for *what*.

"Did you know his position on the Mountain Vista project? Did you ever talk about it?"

Marilyn shook her head. "He'd made a point never to weigh in on Wander Canyon and Mountain Vista. He told me he wanted to stay out of it here. Out of respect for me, and Mom and Dad." It was no secret that Mom and Dad were vocal in their opposition to Mountain Vista, as was most of the Canyon.

Tessa's face grew more serious. "Mari, Landon was actually involved with Mountain Vista. He'd been working with them. He's been in league with them for years."

Some tiny, persistent shred of optimism wanted to say she was surprised. That her belief in Landon hadn't dissolved that far. But the sad truth was that it didn't really surprise her. It felt good to believe he'd stayed clear of Wander Canyon out of respect for her and her family, so she believed it. She believed his lie that he'd kept his business dealings in Denver or elsewhere.

And now his lie had followed her here. Marilyn swallowed hard, pressing her palms against the table for support. "How?"

"Well, I don't really know yet, but the Denver reporter showed me a bunch of strategy emails. Talking about how to win over the community, which ranches to make offers on, which banks would reveal who was behind on their mortgages, that sort of thing." Tessa pulled the papers out. "They got their hands on some incriminating emails." She pointed to a memo listing an email address Marilyn had never seen Landon use.

The fact that Landon had secret email addresses ought to be a slap of shock. Only it wasn't. It simply added to the slipping sensation of fear, the fragile bridge to life beyond Landon now starting its collapse around her.

Tessa went on, her voice filled with both regret and concern. "These aren't nice emails. And the Denver paper is planning on publishing some of them. His name is going to get dragged up in this."

Landon was usually very savvy about covering his tracks. *Lord, I turned a blind eye. I told myself I was wrong even when I knew I wasn't.* She'd fought to cling to the idea of the charming visionary she thought she'd married. The man who went to church and gave to charity and brought her flowers for no reason. Even as she slowly became aware of his questionable dealings, Marilyn convinced herself to ignore what Landon called "necessary alignments."

"It's just part of getting business done," he'd said. "The cost of gaining the power to do what's right." In the final year, Landon's duplicity and inattention had strangled whatever love she had for him. The terrible truth was that whatever faith Landon had possessed when they were married had evaporated in front of her eyes the minute men of power had taken notice of him. It was the parable of the sower played out right in front of her—seeds choked out by the thorns of "cares of this world and the deceitfulness of riches."

When she dared to raise any concerns, he dismissed them. "Why can't you support me?" he'd challenge. "Look at all the things I give you and the girls."

"I don't want things!" she'd shouted back one night. "I want the man I married. The one who loves his family. I want him back."

He'd stormed out that night, and stayed out. When he failed to come home, Marilyn thought her marriage had hit a new low.

When a pair of police officers came to the door just after dawn, she learned not only had her marriage ended, but Landon's life, as well. It had taken a lot of pleading and a full-court press of the law firm's influence to keep his blood alcohol levels out of the newspaper accounts of his car crash. Every cell in her body remembered what dread felt like, and the sensation returned too easily.

"Mari?" Tessa's hand was on hers, pulling Marilyn back to the present. "I'm so sorry about this. It must be a shock."

Marilyn rose and went to the fridge. She needed to move, to make her limbs work, prove her dread hadn't swallowed her. She froze with her hand on the fridge door, unable to open it or return to the table.

"Oh, dear," she said, just because it sounded like what she was supposed to say. She remembered reading somewhere that mortal wounds never actually hurt, that the body went into a numbing shock. That's what this felt like. Or ought to have felt like, if she'd felt anything at all. Dread should feel hot and menacing like fire, but it had always felt cold and numb.

A burst of the girls' laughter came in through the open kitchen window, and it sliced through her. *This is how it starts. One day too soon they'll know. They'll realize who—and what—their father was.* The wall she'd tried to build around them was starting to fall. *Oh, dear Lord,* she moaned silently in prayer, her knuckles white as she clutched the refrigerator handle. *How do I go from here? How do I watch this happen? How will You protect us?*

Tessa came up behind her, placing a hand on her shoulder. "So you didn't know?" The kindness in her voice made it all so much worse. People wouldn't be kind for long. The short bursts of sympathy would give way to stares and avoided conversations. *"That's her. She was married to that man. Those are his girls, you know."* Maybe someone like Wyatt Walker could fend that off all his life, but she wasn't that strong. Not anymore.

In a tiny pop of tragic logic, one item for her list of blessings surfaced. *We haven't bought a house yet. It'll make it easier to go someplace else.*

"I knew Landon wasn't perfect," Marilyn replied. The understatement tasted sour—too much like something the law firm publicity office would have said. She had to will her fingers to let go of the handle, not even bothering with the pretense of opening it. "But no, I didn't know."

"Nothing's concrete in terms of proof…yet." Tessa's shrug told Marilyn they both knew the eventuality of that. Landon was involved with Mountain Vista. It was only a question of how deep—and how legal. That might have left room for innocence with other men, but Marilyn knew this was the beginning of the end for Landon. And likely for her and the twins.

Chapter Eleven

He had no business being here.

Wyatt sat with his truck running, staring at the entrance to the long driveway to Marilyn's parents' house. It was one of those postcard Colorado homes, rustic and yet scrupulously tidy. Not as big as the compound on Wander Canyon Ranch, but with a generous yard and set in the nicest part of town. While she hadn't talked about it much, Wyatt got the sense that she saw her parents' home as confining. He certainly knew a bit about familial homes coming with pressure and expectations.

Still, Maddie and Margie had boasted about the new swing set that had been delivered last week. So did that mean Marilyn and the girls planned to stay here for a while and not look for their own place? Were swing sets portable? He didn't know. He wasn't the kind of guy who would know stuff like that. Which is exactly what kept him from turning into the drive.

It was Saturday, the day Marilyn had said she and the girls were coming to the garage. Only they hadn't appeared, and somehow he knew that meant something. Something good? Something bad? He'd tried to brush it off, busying himself with garage business, but it hadn't taken his mind off Marilyn, and the crazy worry that wouldn't leave him.

Marilyn's car was parked beside the garage, so he could be reasonably sure she was home. If her mom and dad were there, however, this could get a bit prickly. He could only guess they wouldn't take to the local bad boy showing up unannounced to see their daughter, grown woman or not. They'd fend him off, so showing up unannounced was the only way he'd get to see her. And he *needed* to see her. Even if only to convince himself she was fine.

What was happening to him? Since when was he willing to waltz into a house of upturned noses just to see if a woman was okay? He tried to tell himself this was about the girls, but that was a joke. It was about them, partly, but it was more about Marilyn. Since the Mountain Vista conversation with Tim—and a fruitless pair of hours trying to wade through the garage paperwork without Marilyn—he'd come to a decision. He was going to look into this dyslexia thing. He'd been waiting to tell her that in person, and still wanted to, only she hadn't shown.

If you want to tell her, you have to go up to that door, he told himself. So Wyatt called upon his legendary defiant nature, drove up the curving gravel drive and rang Marilyn Sofitel's doorbell.

Marilyn's mother came to the door. Katie Ralton's polite smile barely hid her suspicious expression. "Wyatt," she said tightly. "We weren't expecting a visit from you this afternoon."

Not exactly a warm welcome. Still, he wasn't going to let this woman make him feel like some teenager late to pick up a date. He applied a charming smile to let the woman know he wasn't put off by her frosty greeting. "I was stopping by to see Marilyn and the girls. They didn't come by the garage this morning."

Katie arched one gray eyebrow. "Were you expecting them?"

Now that was a loaded question, wasn't it? "She had said she and the twins were coming by, and it's not like her to not show without calling, is it? I see her car's out front. Is she home?" Behind Katie he heard the sound of Maddie's and Margie's voices, which told him the likely answer.

Maddie appeared behind her grandmother. The way her brown eyes lit up at the sight of Wyatt only emphasized how cold Katie's welcome had been. "Mr. Wyatt!" Maddie shouted happily, dodging around her grandmother's legs to give Wyatt a great big hug. Her enthusiasm sank straight to his heart despite the rather stunned look on Katie's face.

Maddie turned her face back into the house and yelled "Mom! Margie! Mr. Wyatt's here!"

Katie frowned. Wyatt simply shrugged and offered a wider grin.

Admitting defeat, she stepped aside. "Why don't you come in? Mari's on the deck reading."

By the time he'd made it to the back deck of the house, the girls had run to tell Marilyn and she stood at the large glass sliding doors that led out onto the beautiful deck. The view from here was just as stunning as the one he always loved from the deck on Wander Ranch. Familiar gorgeous mountains and crystal-clear skies framed Marilyn as she stood there.

Something was wrong. Really wrong. She looked caved in on herself, despite her carefully applied smile.

"Hi, Mr. Wyatt," Margie greeted. "Look at our new swing set!"

"It's a beauty," Wyatt agreed. "You can show me how it works…in a bit."

Maddie rolled her eyes. "You *know* how a swing set works. Everybody does."

"Yeah, maybe. Just give me a minute with your mom then, okay? I'll come see it in a sec."

Thankfully, the girls accepted that and trotted off toward the play set. That departure didn't buy him much privacy, however, because Wyatt had no doubt Katie was watching him from the kitchen window.

He leaned in as much as he dared. "You didn't come to the garage. Are you okay?"

"Sorry. I should have called. I'm fine." Her words were clipped, and she cast a quick glance over his shoulder toward the kitchen windows behind him.

No way was she okay. "You sure?"

She pivoted toward the yard, and Wyatt wondered if she was turning away from the house or toward the girls. "I was a little tired, that's all." She wrapped her arms around her chest. "Any progress on the carousel?"

So we're not gonna talk about it. "That new part just might do the trick."

"You're doing a good thing there, Wyatt. You're a good man."

As much as he liked hearing such praise from her, there was an undeniable touch of something—sadness? regret?—behind her words.

Wyatt took a small step closer to her. "Mari," he said, taking the risk of using the name she'd used in high school. "Tell me what's wrong. Please."

She turned toward him, eyes suddenly sharp. "I'm a widow with two young girls. Of course something's wrong. *Everything's* still wrong." As quickly as the outburst had come, her face tightened and he watched her shut herself back up. She gripped the handrail and one hand went over her eyes. "I'm sorry. You didn't deserve that. It's just… I'm…" She gave a sigh that was so full of weariness it made his chest hurt. "I still have bad days, you know?"

She was so good at putting up the happy front for the girls, he'd forgotten how much Marilyn must have loved Landon. He hadn't been gone even a year, and he was the father of her children. And not that love ever made much sense—Dad and Chaz were prime examples of that—but he still couldn't see her with a guy like Sofitel. Out of curiosity, he'd looked into the guy. Landon Sofitel was all slick ambition. A real up-and-comer with a shiny life probably lots of people envied.

While Marilyn had struck him as the shiny-life type at first, she didn't seem that way at all now that he knew her. Wyatt couldn't shake the feeling that what he saw in her eyes wasn't so much grief as it was fear. The way she always looked around, the way she wrung her hands and tried *so hard* to look happy, gave off an anxious vigilance that never seemed to leave her. That spooked edge seemed to swallow her whole today, and it drove him nuts that she wouldn't let him help.

So he gave her the only boost he could. "I wanted to tell you. I made an appointment with the learning center over at WCC."

He was glad to see it bring a tiny bit of warmth back to her eyes. "You did?"

"I figured I might as well see if you were right. Maybe they'll help me even more than you have." He couldn't tell if thanking her for her suggestion would make things better or worse. "There's a job at Mountain Vista a friend wants to get me in for, but it's got all kinds of paperwork involved."

She literally winced at the name of the resort. What was up with that? "You know me and paperwork," he joked, unsure how to handle her reaction. "I can't exactly bring my helpers along to a place like that."

It seemed the wrong thing to say, although he was clueless as to why.

"I'm happy for you." Her words rang hollow and forced. He'd meant the news to make her happy, to let her know she'd been right to meddle, but it was as if he couldn't crack the wall she'd thrown up in front of herself.

"Are you sure you're okay?" He had the crazy urge to take her hand.

"You don't need to keep asking that, all right?"

"Yeah," he relented. "Sorry." He backpedaled to safer ground. "Nice swing set." That felt like useless small talk, but he wasn't about to admit defeat and leave. There had to be something he could do, and he wasn't about to let Granny Scowlface back at the kitchen window think she'd won.

"We just put it up, too."

Her wistful tone caught Wyatt up short. "Wait... Are you leaving?"

She shook her head no, but he didn't believe it. It only told him that if she was leaving, it wasn't by choice.

"Come push us on the swings, Mr. Wyatt!" Maddie called from the yard.

Wyatt held up a hand that he'd heard them. "In a minute, okay?" He turned toward her. Women came in and out of his life with a practiced ease, so the sharp prick at the thought of losing her and the girls startled him. He reached his hand toward her elbow. "Mari, please. Tell me what's going on."

She pulled in the smallest of breaths, and after a half a second of connection he knew they both felt, she pulled away.

Touching her—even just the smallest bit—unleashed some strange, tender urge that felt as un-Wyatt as anything. Defiance he knew well. But this weird protective thing? This *you can't hurt her* battle cry that came out of nowhere? It stumped him worse than a dozen broken carousels.

"Aren't you gonna come push us?" the girls called insistently.

She turned to him with eyes that held back tears. "Whatever you read, whatever you hear, don't..." She never finished the sentence, just clamped her mouth shut.

Wyatt turned to fully face her, not caring who watched. "Don't what? Mari..."

"We're coming!" Marilyn called with a desperate cheer. "We'll come push you on your swings."

Wyatt wanted to growl in frustration, but instead he walked down the deck stairs behind Marilyn to go push two little girls on the brand-new swing set. He'd said what he'd come to say, but he'd leave with far more questions and a lot more worry.

Maddie pulled her blanket up tight and clutched her stuffed animal. "I love our new swings."

Marilyn viewed the brightly colored play set as a planted flag of victory, a tiny bit of surefire happiness. At least for now. That, and the fact that she'd gotten called in for an interview with a local manufacturing firm, had to be enough good news to live on. "They are fun, aren't they?"

"Can we go back to the garage next week?" Margie asked with a yawn. "Mr. Wyatt says he missed us."

Marilyn smoothed the girl's hair back, still damp and sweet smelling from the evening's bath. "Oh, I don't know. We'll see." The urge to hide out here at Mom and Dad's house hit hard. It could be days, or months, or hours until whatever the Denver paper was planning to write hit the news, if it ever did at all. She couldn't live the rest of her life waiting for the ax to fall. She had to make a life beyond Landon. She just wasn't sure she could get beyond Landon. And Wander was always watching.

He'd left so many buried land mines behind. In Denver, and now here. It gave an irrational lure to the thought of piling suitcases into the car and running somewhere far away. Marilyn wondered, at that moment, if she'd subconsciously put up the swing set to make it harder to leave.

Maddie flipped on her side on the twin bed a few feet away. "'We'll see' always means 'no.'"

"Not always," she countered, again wondering where Maddie got these flashes of entirely too-grown-up wisdom. When Maddie gave her a "really?" look, Marilyn added, "Just most of the time."

"I still wanna go," Margie said. "Mr. Wyatt says he's worried he'll get homework from the learning center like me."

She'd been surprised when Wyatt told her he was making an appointment at the church's learning center about the possibility of his having dyslexia. She'd been flat-out shocked when he told Margie, asking her if she'd show him the ropes. Whether or not he accepted whatever assessment the learning center offered Wyatt, Margie's eyes at being asked to help a grown-up would warm her heart for years. For a man who adamantly claimed kids weren't his thing, he sure had a way with them that went far beyond carousels.

Wyatt saw the twins as people, as individual personalities. Not everyone did. Landon had treated the girls as a set, or as a novelty. Disloyal as it felt to admit, she'd always felt Landon merely loved the idea of having twins. His affection never seemed to truly extend to the girls as two unique and precious daughters. He never spent time one-on-one with them. He never spent much time at all with any of them.

In fact, it broke her heart to realize she could not pull up a single memory of Landon pushing the girls on a swing. So now she didn't know what to do with the picture of Wyatt laughing and making jokes and dodging in and out of the swings as if it was the most fun he'd had in years. Wyatt Walker, whose reckless exploits had fueled school gossip, who totaled a car an hour before prom and simply regrouped to take his date to the dance on the back of his motorcycle.

Wyatt Walker, whose heart-stopping eyes had held her gaze for far too long and said a million things without words before he got back into his truck and drove off.

"Do you, Mom?" Margie was tugging on her hand, pulling her back from her thoughts.

"Do I what?"

"Do you think Mr. Wyatt is nice?"

Marilyn tried not to let the question throw her. "I think everybody is nice. I mean, Greg pushed you on the swings the other day, too, didn't he?"

Maddie grunted. "His mom made him."

"Who told you that?" Marilyn asked.

"He did. He got pizza if he did it."

Ah, teenagers. They had all the tact of a Wander Canyon Ranch steer. "Well, I think you're worth four pizzas." She was pleased that made the girls giggle.

"So, do you?" Margie's persistence might also rival a Wander Canyon Ranch steer.

She opted for the safest answer she could think of. "He's been very nice to us, hasn't he?"

"I like helping in the garage. Can I draw him another picture tomorrow?"

There was something wonderful about how Margie never hesitated to share her art with the world. "I don't see why not."

"We can give it to him on our next visit. Can't we go tomorrow?"

Marilyn wasn't sure she was ready to face Wyatt again. She didn't want to face anyone. She wanted to hide under a rock until no one had any more secrets to expose about Landon. It felt as if the man she grieved as her husband didn't even exist anymore. Did he ever? The swirl of doubts made her as dizzy. "I really don't know. Let's think about this tomorrow, okay? It's time for two little girls to say their prayers and go to sleep."

The moments where Margie and Maddie ended their days with prayers was always a treasure to Marilyn's heart. They gave thanks for the sweetest—and often strangest—things. Tonight Margie thanked God for earthworms and peanut butter—and Mr. Wyatt's funny jokes. Maddie gave thanks for hair bows and Grandpa's tickles. When each girl asked God to bless Daddy in heaven, Marilyn's heart twisted in both regret and gratitude. Could their unvarnished memory of their father have any hope of staying that way? *Their happiness means so much to me,* she pleaded to Heaven as she kissed each forehead and switched off the light.

She stopped at the top of the landing, continuing her prayer. *I feel like a great big storm is coming that I can't stop. Be my protector, Lord. Grant me wisdom and courage.* And finally, she admitted, *Show me what to do about Wyatt. I can't trust all the things I'm feeling. The girls are hungry for attention. We're all in such a vulnerable place. Guide us through this, I beg You.*

While some part of her yearned to go crawl under

the covers herself, Marilyn settled for heading downstairs for a cup of tea and the chance to finish a few
rows on the scarf she'd started knitting. Mom had encouraged her to take the craft back up, and she welcomed the chance to share something with her mother.
She hadn't told Mom and Dad anything about what
Tessa had shared. They'd know soon enough. For now,
the peace of a few quietly accomplished rows on the
back deck under an indigo summer night sky with a
cup of tea sounded like just the balm she needed.

She winced at the sight of the papers on the kitchen
table—Mom and Dad read the *Wander Gazette* when it
came out twice a week as well as the *Denver Courier*
daily. Marilyn tried to ignore them as she walked out
onto the deck with her cup of tea. Mom and Dad sat
on the deck with a cheery fire roaring in the fire pit.

"Girls all tucked in?" Dad asked, stretching out his
legs. His knee was bothering him again, she could tell.
An irrational chill of *what will happen when they're
gone and I'm all alone?* shot through her. Some days
grief was just a hailstorm of hard emotions coming
up out of nowhere, and today was surely one of those.

"Maddie thanked God for your tickles tonight," she
shared, pleased at her father's resulting smile. "And
Margie for your peanut butter sandwiches," she added,
not wanting to leave Mom out even though Margie
hadn't been that specific. They never spoke of it, but
Marilyn knew it had to be a burden of sorts to have
her and a pair of loud, messy children invade her parents' quiet retirement.

"What did Wyatt Walker want?" Mom's attempt to
keep the question casual didn't quite succeed. She re-

turned to her knitting as she asked, "Didn't you just see him the other day?"

Marilyn opted for the truth—or at least part of it. "He expected to see us at the garage today and was worried when we didn't show up."

"He *expected* you?" Her mother's eyebrows furrowed with her emphasis of the word. "Awfully strange place for girls that age, don't you think? All that machinery."

"He made paths and safe places for them to walk and sit and watch with yellow tape on the floor." She'd found it charming, but the moment the words left her mouth Marilyn realized how ridiculous that must sound. Who tries to childproof an auto garage?

She picked up her own knitting. At the slow rate she was going, it might take her until Christmas to get this purple scarf done for Margie and a second pink one for Maddie.

After a stretch of silence, Dad said, "You be careful." His eyes told her he meant it in more ways than one.

Marilyn returned the knitting to her lap. "You know, Dad, I think he's dyslexic. I saw lots of the same problems Margie has when I helped him with the garage paperwork. I gave him some information and he's going to get evaluated at the church learning center. You should have seen how sweet he was to ask Margie if she'd show him the ropes." She wasn't entirely sure that was her secret to tell, but the way Mom looked as if Wyatt was some bandit worthy of scorn made her blurt it out.

Mom turned her work with a small harrumph. "I

don't see why you have to get wrapped up in something like that."

"I'm not wrapped up in anything."

Oh, but she was. She didn't know what to do with the way she felt around Wyatt, with how much the girls had grown to like him. She was wrapped up in some unwelcome desire to be closer to him, in the comfort and freedom that messy garage somehow gave her.

Tangled might be the better word. And when whatever was coming out about Landon finally surfaced, those tangles felt like they would tighten into knots.

Chapter Twelve

Someone was shaking her shoulder. "Mari, hon, wake up."

Marilyn had terrible trouble getting to sleep last night. The sweetness and innocence of the girls' prayers kept clashing with her pain and fear, keeping her spirit in turmoil until the wee hours of Saturday morning. She must have slept in and the girls needed something.

"Get up, Mari." Her father's voice held an edge that made Marilyn's stomach drop even before she fully opened her eyes.

"What? The girls?" As she lifted her head from the pillow, she realized it wasn't late at all. In fact, it seemed to be rather early. The ache in her body told her she'd been asleep only a handful of hours. "Are they okay?"

"They're still asleep. But you need to come downstairs. Coffee's on and we're going to have to figure out what to do."

A sensation of a threatening *thunk*, like a heavy

lock clicking into place, filled her chest. *It's done. It's happened. Already.* For no logical reason she'd thought she'd have more time. But when were scandals ever slow-moving? No, they took on wildfire speed once the match was struck. She started to reach for her cell phone charging on the nightstand, but Dad's hand stopped her. "Let's not do that yet."

Marilyn sat straight up, wide awake. "Dad, what's going on?"

He straightened up. "Just come on downstairs. We'll take it one step at a time from here."

"Landon?" The name seemed to burst out of her. "It's about Landon, isn't it?"

Dad showed a moment of surprise at her guess, making her wonder if it had been the right choice to not tell Mom and Dad what Tessa had said was coming. He merely handed her the robe from the foot of the bed and gave a small nod. "Coffee's on."

Marilyn stopped in the bathroom to splash some water on her face, then felt her chest tighten as she padded past the half-shut door to the girls' room. The stars of their night-light cast yellow reassurance onto the walls. *Oh, Lord,* was the only prayer she could manage, and not much of one at that.

The kitchen lights were fully on, not just the table lamp Mom usually lit this early in the morning. Dad handed her a cup of coffee. Mom sat with both hands wrapped around her mug. A copy of the Sunday *Denver Courier* lay open on the table. It didn't take long for Marilyn's eyes to find the words *Mountain Vista* among the headlines.

She should have told them. She should have warned

them. But then again, wouldn't that only rush the pain toward them? After all, what could any of them have done?

Mom's eyes were unreadable—half wonder, half suspicion. "Did you know?"

The fact that Mom could have been talking about half a dozen things rung hollow and foreboding in Marilyn's chest. She could have unloaded about all that she suspected in the months before Landon died, but she chose to start with the facts she knew. "It's what Tessa came to tell me."

"How did Tessa know?" Dad asked.

"There was a *Courier* reporter digging around on the Mountain Vista issue. They wanted our local paper's cooperation. Landon's name had come up. She told me it wasn't—" Marilyn ran her hands over her eyes, still not yet wide enough awake to really take it all in "—kind. But the details… I knew some." She looked at her dad. "But I'm pretty sure there's more."

Dad sat down. "Well, now everyone does. They're saying Landon has been working with Mountain Vista to size up and buy land for four years. If not longer."

"Four years?" She hadn't even bothered to look at the date on the memo Tessa had shown her. Somehow none of the details seemed to matter now that the floodgate was open. Did it really matter how long Landon had been conspiring with Mountain Vista? The first rancher had sold out to the resort about two years ago. Marilyn pulled the paper toward her, catching sight of an article sidebar labeled "Bovine to Botox? MV's Aggressive Plans to Expand." The article's first few paragraphs quoted some of the leaked memos Tessa had. The language accused Mountain Vista of plans to ruthlessly gobble up most of the canyon in order to expand, but that wasn't news. What was news was how the article went on to talk about "sly use of local influencers." It named a few names, but only one with direct connections to Wander Canyon. "Landon Sofitel, husband of lifelong Wander resident Marilyn Ralton Sofitel, deftly gained community trust, secured inside information on potential ranches vulnerable to sale and secretly pressed for needed zone modifications."

There it was. Landon's name *and* hers. It didn't matter that his wasn't the only name mentioned. Nor did it matter that no one seemed to be sure if whatever Landon had done was illegal or merely unethical. It looked wrong, felt wrong, would be perceived as wrong. And she was attached to it in front of the whole world.

Marilyn didn't know what to say. She didn't know how to meet the questions in her parents' eyes. "Landon did business with all kinds of people. I never knew half of them." Shame heated her cheeks. "In the last year I started to have…questions. He'd talk about connections he needed to make if he was going to launch a Senate run. He started to have an—" she fumbled for a way to describe it "—edge to him I didn't like. Preoccupied and demanding. We used to talk about everything and it slowly stopped." She couldn't figure out how to communicate her innocence without sounding clueless. Maybe it couldn't be done. Maybe she was merely waking up to the fact that her own husband, the father of her children, had fooled her like he fooled everyone else.

Mom's jaw clenched. "People will believe this." The words held a desperate hope that there might still be a chance it wasn't true.

Marilyn no longer had that hope. She held her mother's tight gaze. "I think it's true. It's at least possible."

Mom picked up her coffee mug. "That man was your husband." Marilyn couldn't tell if her mother meant *you should defend him* or *you should have known better* by her statement.

The deeper truth she'd been trying not to reveal to Mom and Dad came tumbling out of her. "Landon changed. By the time he died he wasn't the man I married." She stopped just short of saying "He wasn't the man I fell in love with." Whether or not she loved him felt totally beside the point this morning. Her last name was Sofitel now. Margie and Maddie bore that name. That name was in the papers. The dread she'd felt nipping at her heels for months now was out and roaring, ready to eat her alive. Marilyn's spine iced over with the knowledge that this was likely to be only the first of many revelations. Public opinion loved a pile-on, and Wander was always watching.

Landon Sofitel may have started out a good man, but he didn't die one. And now the whole world would discover it right alongside her. She could claim she didn't know, but would it matter? At all?

Dad laid his hand on top of hers. "Mari, honey, why on earth are we hearing about this now? If you were unhappy, why haven't you said anything before?" He squeezed her hand into his. "Why at least didn't you come to us Thursday when Tessa warned you?"

Mom set down her coffee mug. "Did *he* know? Didn't you say he was applying for some job with that company?" She said it as if the she couldn't even bear speaking the name *Mountain Vista*.

It took a minute for Marilyn to work out that her mother was talking about Wyatt. "What's Wyatt got to do with this?"

"He showed up demanding to speak to you the day after Tessa visited, didn't he? Wanting to know if you were okay?"

It was all right there in Mom's tone. Suspicion caught like a wildfire in these parts, burning things down at the slightest association. She'd be viewed as part of Landon's scheme, and whether she ever was wouldn't matter at all. Mom, for all her split-second condemnation, wasn't wrong. She could hear the voices already. *"Poor Ed and Katie. Their daughter married that Sofitel scoundrel, didn't she? Shame no one caught on."*

The phone rang despite the early hour. Mom looked as if it was the first drop of a torrential rainstorm. Dad merely sighed and picked up the receiver.

"Hello, Pastor." Pause. "Yes," he said wearily. "We have. Only just."

Mom's eyes squinted shut.

After a pause, Dad said, "No, I don't think that's necessary just yet. Why don't you stop by later in the day. We're still just sorting things out over here." Another pause. "Much appreciated. No, she's just awake now. We're talking things over. I'll tell her. Thanks."

Dad looked at her as he hung up the phone. "What are we going to do now?"

Marilyn gave the only answer she had. "I don't know."

Wyatt had never had a job interview on a Sunday morning on a golf cart before, but it beat a weekday interview, filling out a pile of forms in some cubicle. The unconventional setting and timing made Wyatt think maybe working for Mountain Vista wouldn't be such a bad idea after all.

They weren't actually playing golf—Wyatt had never taken up the game, which thankfully Tim told him wouldn't matter. They were simply touring the nine holes Mountain Vista had up and running now as Tim laid out the firm's plans for four golf courses over the next few years. "Things are a bit nuts at the office right now with the press that came out this morning. I figured it'd be easier out here," Tim said as he steered the little vehicle around a curve toward the next hole.

Wyatt never read newspapers. "Good PR day?"

Tim laughed. "Hardly. *The Courier* came out with some piece on our land purchases. You know, the stuff everyone always complains about. Folks never like progress if it lands in their own backyard."

Wyatt elbowed his friend. "You mean if it steals their backyard."

"Bought. At a fair price," Tim corrected.

Wyatt knew most people in Wander Canyon would take issue with that particular statement.

They were about to round a set of shrubs when loud voices stopped them. "You told me Sofitel could be discreet!" one voice shouted. "You told me he wouldn't leave loose ends like those memos hanging around!"

"Oops," Tim whispered, moving to turn the vehicle around. "Thought we'd be more alone out here."

"Well, he hardly kept up his end, did he?" the voice continued.

Wyatt held out a hand to stop him. Tim gave him a "huh?" look, but kept the cart still.

"He did," came the other voice. "The guy married a local. How much more did you want him to do?"

Wyatt's gut went off like an alarm bell. He slipped out of the cart and edged up to the bushes to view two older men squaring off over their golf bags.

"Well, look at all the good it did us," said the nearer one. "Our guy on the inside up and got himself killed, and now all his dirty laundry comes out. Linked straight to us." He shoved the club he was holding back into the bag. "I told Landon they should have lived here rather than Denver, but no. He kept insisting it was enough that he married her."

"Well, that was the deal, wasn't it?" the second man replied. "He establishes himself as one of them, we back him for the Senate seat. If you ask me, he did keep up his end of the deal."

The first man just grunted.

"Family man, twins and all," the first man went on. "He was heading downhill when he died, you know that."

"The DUI," the other one agreed. "And that business with the secretary."

Wyatt nearly winced from the stabbing feeling in his chest. He was glad the man hadn't felt the need to elaborate. It didn't take much of an imagination to guess the details. The wounded look in Marilyn's eyes made sense now. It had been a while since Wyatt felt such a powerful urge to punch something. Or someone. Landon Sofitel ended his time on earth as a first-class jerk. He hoped for Marilyn's sake that Landon hadn't started out that way, that he'd been some type of husband and father to his family.

The men started climbing back in their golf cart. "Hey, the way I figure it, we dodged a bullet. And besides—all that young-widow sympathy? It could work in our favor here."

Wyatt found himself glad the men were driving away from him, because he wanted to stomp through the bushes and tell those idiots to stop talking about Marilyn as if she was a promotional asset. She was a grieving mother. A widow. How low could these types go in pursuit of a profit?

"Like I said," Tim offered. "We're out here because things are a bit tense at the office today. But you know what they say—the only bad press is no press."

Wyatt merely grunted, unsure of a safe reply given the anger clanging around in his chest at the moment. And then it came to him, clear as the morning air. He looked at Tim. His friend seemed taken aback by having stumbled onto a private conversation, but oblivious as to what Wyatt considered the despicable nature of the conversation. He'd known Tim half his life, but suddenly felt as if he didn't know the man sitting next to him at all.

He looked around at the neatly tended grounds, the fancy golf cart, the high-end coffee drinks Tim had brought for them from the course's espresso bar. What was he doing here? On this cart on some ritzy golf course? He looked at the Mountain Vista logo on the golf cart, on Tim's shirt, even on the paper coffee cups. This wasn't him. He wasn't a corporation guy. He wasn't even an office guy. Why had he made this move toward something he never really wanted?

Wyatt no longer wanted to be out here at all. "You know what? I think we're done here."

Tim balked at him. "What do you mean?"

"I'm not your guy."

"Hey, don't let those two guys spook you. It's just a bit of bad press. They told us to expect some push-back." Tim looked at him. "Wait...you don't... Mari Ralton..."

"Marilyn *Sofitel*," Wyatt corrected with emphasis. As in the local they were just talking about."

"C'mon," Tim scoffed. "It'll all blow over and you can laugh at the critics from your shiny new truck."

Wyatt shook his head. "Nope. I'm done." He wanted to go find Marilyn and stand guard between her and anyone clucking their tongues this morning. He didn't know what the *Courier* had written, but it didn't matter.

Tim slammed the golf cart into gear. "I stuck my neck out for you. Really, Walker, since when do you care what people think?"

"This isn't about what anyone thinks of me."

"I don't know what's gotten into you, man."

Not what, Wyatt thought. *Who.*

Tim dropped Wyatt off at his truck—a perfectly fine shiny truck he already owned—and stomped off with a few choice words about Wyatt's ungrateful attitude. Wyatt hoped the longtime friendship hadn't just ended, but couldn't ignore that he'd just met a Tim he hadn't seen before. Maybe one he should have seen coming.

Then again, who had really changed? Tim or himself?

He stalked around the truck for a moment, not quite sure of his next move. The only clear thought pounding in his head was a burning need to protect Marilyn and the girls. But from what? And how? At a loss for a better plan, he dialed Marilyn's cell phone.

"Wyatt?"

He hated how frail her voice sounded. "Are you okay? I mean, I haven't seen whatever's in the papers but I know it isn't good."

"How?"

Because a couple of jerks were dragging the Sofitel name through the mud a minute ago. "Who cares how? Where are you?"

"At home. Where are you?"

He couldn't stomach telling her he was at Mountain Vista. "I'm heading to the garage. You could bring the girls there… If you need to…get away." It wasn't really a sensible suggestion except he needed to see her and he didn't think Ed and Katie would be too keen on visitors—especially him—right now.

"I don't know." Marilyn's damp, doubtful sniff went right through his ribs. She'd been crying. What was in those papers? "Going into town feels…"

"I'll open the bay door and you can pull right in. No one will know you're there. Let me help, Marilyn." A surprising thought struck him. "Or go to Dad's ranch. I can meet you there if that feels better. You don't really want to stay at the house with your folks right now, do you?"

She lowered her voice. "Well, no."

Dad would just have to get over his shock that he was bringing Marilyn Sofitel and her girls to the ranch. If home really was the place where they had to take you in, today seemed like a good day to test the theory. "Head to Wander Canyon Ranch, Mari. I'll be there." He pushed the anger out of his voice, softening it as much as he was able. "Let me do this for you. For the girls."

"Okay."

Chapter Thirteen

The Wander Canyon Ranch kitchen smelled of coffee and pancakes when Wyatt pushed through the door a few minutes later.

Pauline looked up from her breakfast, rightfully surprised at his entrance. "Wyatt! Your father's—"

He cut her off. "Marilyn Sofitel and her girls will be here in a few minutes on account of—" he noticed the Sunday paper folded open to an article with Mountain Vista in the headline "—that."

"Oh, my." Pauline took it all in, then seemed to shift into gear. "Well, your father's in the barn," She opened a kitchen cabinet. "Will the girls want breakfast?"

What time was it, anyway? "I suppose. I didn't really have a plan when I told them to come." Wyatt turned in a slow circle, hands raking through his hair. He suddenly had no idea what he was doing or why he was here.

Pauline filled a mug of coffee and handed it to him as she nodded toward the paper. "She's got to be devastated by all that."

He didn't even really know what "all that" was yet. What he'd heard from the men on the golf course was bad enough. What was in the papers? He remembered Marilyn's words to him from yesterday at the swing set. *"Whatever you read, whatever you hear..."* She'd known it was coming.

"They're welcome here," Pauline said, one hand on Wyatt's arm. "As are you."

There had been weeks in his recent past where Wyatt hadn't felt welcome here. Only home didn't stop being home just because you hated it. And he'd never really hated it, just the pressure of doing something he never seemed meant to do. Funny how Pauline—his father's new wife—and Marilyn and the twins had gotten him to that realization. He didn't have much to give Mari and the girls, but if he could extend the refuge that was Wander Canyon Ranch, then he'd endure whatever odd looks came from this morning's unlikely appearance.

The door opened behind him to reveal Chaz and Yvonne. "I saw Wyatt's truck come in."

"Mari and the girls will be here in a few minutes." Wyatt offered, as if it explained everything. Which, of course, it didn't. Not by a long shot.

"Here?" Yvonne asked. She had every right to be surprised not only that Wyatt was here, but that he'd invited guests. "Why?"

Pauline simply held up the newspaper. "Seems we make an excellent hideout. What's wrong with Ed and Katie's place that Marilyn has to hide here?"

Wyatt shut his eyes and gulped down his coffee as Yvonne skimmed the article. He probably should do the same before Marilyn got here, but he had no hope of reading something that fast. Then again, what was in there didn't matter half as much as what she knew and he'd just heard. "Can we please just forget my massive shortcomings and be nice to her and her girls? She needs a place to think this through. I need a place to think this through." The raised eyebrow Chaz gave him at that last remark made Wyatt regret it. Still, he needed to find out what Marilyn knew before he shared anything of what he'd overheard on the golf course. And he couldn't do that with the girls around.

Wyatt walked over to Pauline. "Can you and Yvonne... I don't know...play with Cecil?" Chaz's dog was good with kids. "Bake something with the girls? Anything so I can talk to Mari alone?"

"What's going on between you two?" Chaz asked pointedly.

If he knew the answer to that, he'd be a lot calmer than he was right now. "Nothing."

Chaz's expression told Wyatt he didn't believe that for a second, but at least his stepbrother kept his opinion to himself.

The side door swung open and Dad came into the kitchen. "Wyatt's car is out front."

"No kidding," Wyatt said, wishing this hadn't turned into the world's most uncomfortable family meeting. *At least try to be nice.* "G'morning, Dad."

"'Morning to you, too, stranger." Dad's face was at once pleased and puzzled. "There's a car coming up the drive."

Wyatt downed the last of his coffee. "That'll be

Marilyn and the girls." He sent a pleading expression to Yvonne and Pauline. "Please?"

Yvonne shrugged. "Of course. We'll help however we can."

Dad hung his hat on the pegs by the door. "Someone want to tell me what on earth is going on?"

"As soon as I know it myself, Dad." Wyatt reached for the door handle as he heard the crunch of tires on the gravel. "I'll send the girls in and take a walk with Marilyn." He pointed toward the paper. "Hide that, if you don't mind." It struck him as a sick twist that Marilyn's life had been shaken loose by words. By something people read.

He pushed out the door to find Maddie scrambling out of the SUV. "Your cows are funny-looking. Can we see them up close?"

"They're so furry!" Margie said as she climbed out the other side. He was glad to see the girls seemed oblivious to what had happened. Marilyn, on the other hand, looked as if she was barely holding it together. He tried to let his gaze steady her as he accepted hugs from the girls. Their innocent happiness sank to the deepest corners of his chest and made it hard to breathe.

"Head on inside, okay? Ms. Yvonne and my stepmom have stuff in there for you."

Without another word, he took Marilyn's hand and pulled her across the driveway toward the small creek that ran alongside the pasture. She offered no resistance. In fact, she started to cry before they were even fully out of sight of the house.

Once he got her to the quiet little grove, Wyatt

didn't even have to think. He just pulled her into his arms and let her cry. The details could wait. The facts could stand aside until she let out whatever she'd been holding in on behalf of the girls. He felt that wall he'd seen her force up come cracking down around them, felt her fear rise up and make her shake against his chest.

Crying women usually irritated him—mostly because it was usually something he did that made them cry—but this felt altogether different. *Tender* and *honorable* were such gushy words, but they described the sense of pride he felt at being able to be there for her. To stand guard over her while her world fell apart. It shocked him and felt good at the same time. He felt no need to search for the clever remark. In fact, he felt no need to speak at all.

After a long while she pushed off his now-damp chest, sniffling into her shirtsleeve and running embarrassed hands through her hair. She looked undone, and it undid something in him. He realized, in the small act of brushing a lock of hair off her blotchy cheek, that he cared about her. Deeply. Who would have ever thought?

"I'm sorry," she said, her voice thin with embarrassment. She tried to pull away from him, but he refused to let her go. "I can't believe I lost it like that." She looked out over the bubbling stream and the peaceful setting. "I've been terrified of this day for months."

He sat down on the large stone that had been his favorite hiding spot for years, pleased to share it with her. At his gesture of invitation, she sat down next to him and hugged her arms to her chest.

"So you knew?" It was a tricky question, seeing as he didn't actually know what Marilyn knew.

She recoiled at that, pulling her knees up to hug them. "I think on some level I always knew Landon would fall in with whoever would further his career. It was easier to pretend I didn't, though." She looked up at Wyatt, scrambling to explain. "He was so different when I married him. Do you think anyone will believe that?"

Wyatt thought of all the things he'd done to win over a woman, all the things he used to exaggerate or even lie about, and felt the edges of his conscience blacken like burning paper. Landon had bowled her over, swept her off her feet according to plan. It was so easy to see because he'd done it himself. And not on some agenda, but just because he could. Did she know what he now knew? Could he bear to break it to her if she didn't? He knew what it felt like to be merely the means to an end, and it was one of life's deepest cuts.

He settled on the closest thing to the truth he could stomach. "He fooled a lot of people."

"And we all know how people hate to be fooled."

"Nobody's going to put this on you, Mari." It felt like that was what he was supposed to say.

She called him on it. "You don't believe that any more than I do. I'm not to blame, but we both know how this sort of thing sticks. The talking that will stop when I enter the room. The whispers. They'll wonder how much I know, how much I knew *all along*." She gave the last two words a bitter edge.

"Okay, it might be bad at first, but people will find something else to talk about soon enough." He gave her shoulder the smallest of playful bumps. "If you want, I can go do something scandalous by Tuesday. You know, draw their fire."

He hoped to make her laugh, but she only gave a sad little whimper. "Each time Mountain Vista gobbles up a new ranch it will start all over again." She pulled in a breath. "We'll probably have to leave town."

"Don't leave." His plea was instantaneous. Alarmingly close to desperate. "I mean," he backpedaled, "if you leave, they win."

She looked at him with tired eyes. "What does that matter? We've already lost."

Wyatt's expression sharpened. "Lost? You haven't lost anything. Landon took something from you. He did it. Not you. He…" Wyatt pushed up off the rock, pacing the lush grass in front of the picturesque little creek. "He doesn't get to take you down with him. He doesn't deserve to."

The power behind his words shot through her. How long had it been since she felt like anyone was fighting in her corner? Life felt as if the hole Landon left behind was so large it swallowed her up along with it. She didn't feel anything close to brave, or coping, or any of those valiant adjectives people liked to associate with young widows. She was just hanging on. And doing a terrible job of it besides.

Suddenly one secret scrambled to get out of her, clawing its way up from the darkest corner of her heart. "Do you know what's in a box at the top of my closet?"

"Huh?" He stopped his pacing and looked at her,

rightfully stumped by the odd response to what he'd just said.

The panic that had hummed just below her control, the one she'd been fighting on some level for months, finally escaped. "In the back of my closet, in a box with a lock. Do you know what's in there?"

Wyatt stood facing her, somehow sensing the importance of what she was going to say. The green creek bank was such a pretty scene. It felt criminal to let something so ugly out into the world in a spot like this. And yet somehow she couldn't hold it back, even though she'd never told anyone, nor thought she ever would. A deep tremble started in the small of her back and worked its way up her spine alongside the words. "It's a letter. Almost a year old. Written by me. To him. Telling him how unhappy I was. Telling him I wanted to leave him."

She'd said it. Out loud. The only thing darker than who Landon really had been was who she was for wanting to leave him. To break her marriage vows. To walk away, just because she was unhappy. Marilyn waited for the shame to rise up out of the ground and swallow her whole.

"My God," Wyatt said.

"No," she shot back, not bothering to stem the tears that now came. "God was nowhere in it. That's the farthest thing from who God is. Who He'd want me to be."

Wyatt crouched down in front of her, looking up into her face with eyes that said a dozen things. Surprise, defiance, a stunning tenderness, and a care she felt helpless to accept. "You never gave it to him."

"Of course not."

"But you kept it."

She'd never really worked out why. "I suppose I thought it was my weapon against him. If I put down on paper how I really felt but could hang on long enough to never actually give it to him, that made me the better person." It seemed utterly absurd now that she said it out loud.

Wyatt took one of her hands. "You *are* the better person. How can you not see that?"

"How? I mean, which is worse? My wanting to leave him or my not having the strength to even tell him I wanted to?"

He took both her hands now, clasping them tightly. "He didn't deserve you."

"Don't say that. You don't know that."

"I do know that. Even before this morning I knew that. You're amazing. You're all those things you think you aren't. You're strong and you love your amazing girls and you're fighting for their future." He looked down for a minute, and she was grateful to catch her breath out of the powerful pull of his gaze. He shifted his weight, as if readying himself, or deciding something. When he looked back up at her, something had hardened in his eyes. A determination of sorts. "Why did you marry Landon?"

It seemed an odd question. "I loved him. He made all these wonderful promises about what our life would be like together. He was a star, a rising shining star who chose little, ordinary me."

"Why did he marry you?" He said the words slowly, with a strange caution she didn't understand.

"He loved me. He always used to say I was the perfect wife for a hundred reasons." She realized, as the words left her, that she couldn't remember the last time Landon said that to her. Just the opposite, as a matter of fact. He seemed to have a hundred reasons why she didn't measure up.

"Mari." She didn't know how to push back against what the sound of his saying her name did to her. How to stop the glow it had started. "Did you know that one of those reasons was that the honchos at Mountain Vista promised to back his Senate campaign if he married a local girl to grease the wheel for them?"

The tremble from the base of her spine racked through her entire body. Marilyn looked for signs of lying in Wyatt's eyes and found only regret. "That's not true." The words were more of a weak gasp than a loyal wife's declaration.

Wyatt swallowed hard. "Well, I don't know if it's true, but this morning I heard two executives talking out on the golf course at Mountain Vista, and they said just that. The guy said he'd struck a deal with Landon that if he made himself a Wander Canyon local—to pave the way for the resort, I suppose—they'd fund his Senate run."

She wanted to be sure it wasn't true. She craved to know deep down in her bones that Landon's love had always been the fairy tale she'd thought it to be. But the words denying that horrible possibility stayed stuck in her throat, unable to come.

It couldn't be. She couldn't have been used in that way, duped for all those years about something that ought to be so deep-down knowable as whether or not your husband really loved you. Whether the father of your children really loved his family, or just saw them as a means to an end.

She ought to be able to stand up and yell "How dare you!" or some other righteous thing. To point a finger at Wyatt's pained expression and defend her late husband, stand by Maddie and Margie's father. Only the sickening possibility of what Wyatt had said seemed to swirl around her. No amount of dread dampened the fact that it *was* possible. It explained a thousand little details that had poked pinpricks of doubt into her. He used to say the strangest things when he got angry, as if life had cheated him out of some great deal. It couldn't be, could it?

It wasn't one big lie, was it? She had loved Landon. She was sure of that. But she could also no longer deny that somewhere along the line that love had grown cold. Did it make it better or worse to think his affections had simply been calculated all along?

"Mari," came Wyatt's voice out of the storm of emotions surrounding her. "Talk to me. Do you think it's true?"

If it was possible to feel yourself disappear, that's what she felt. As if every breath of air she scraped into her lungs somehow made her less solid. She forced the words out of her mouth. "It could be." Saying them somehow made the whole thing more real, and she felt slightly ill.

"I thought maybe you knew. Or guessed. It didn't sound like things were so perfect between you and Landon, and you blamed yourself so much."

"Everybody will know." The words were somewhere between a gasp and a whisper.

"Not from me they won't. Okay, there's the business stuff in the paper, but no one needs to ever know what I heard this morning."

She gave him a sour look. "They will. Landon's a target now. It will come out. Secrets always do. And we'll go right down with him." She went to pull her hands from his. "All I had to stand on was who he was, who we were, and now that's gone."

Wyatt would not release his grip. Instead, he clasped her hands more tightly, and for a moment Marilyn felt as if they were the only thing keeping her from dissolving into thin air. "That's not true," he declared. "You're so much more than who he was. Look at me. I just walked away when it got tough, but you, you stuck it out. You took whatever it is Landon did and made it a family." He shook her hands as he held them, as if pulling her back from the dread swallowing her. "Why can't you see how strong you are? How you deserve so much more than what Landon did to you?"

She couldn't see it. Not today. Today she wanted to run and hide. The prospect of driving off this ranch and walking into town or church or anywhere knowing what was splayed across the newspaper this morning? She couldn't begin to stomach it.

"I deserved anything people said about me," Wyatt went on. "But you? I won't let them. Give me five minutes with anyone who dares to say one thing about you and the girls. They'll find out what the end of a Walker temper really looks like."

His words sounded brave and wonderful, but they

were useless. If her work in public relations had taught her anything, it was that people loved to pull down a rising star. The revelation of one fault would lead to the hunt for more. And it had become crystal clear that there were plenty to be found about Landon Sofitel.

Suddenly Wyatt was pulling her to her feet. "There's only one thing to do. And we're gonna do it. I may not be good at lot of things, but I'm really good at this."

"What?"

"Defiance. You're looking at Wander Canyon's reigning champion." He paused in thought for a moment. "It's Sunday. Isn't there one of those afternoon outdoor church services at WCC today?"

What did that have to do with anything? "I think so."

"Okay, then. We're going."

She shook her hand. "What? No!"

"Yep. You and I and Margie and Maddie and Dad and Pauline and maybe even Chaz and Yvonne. You're gonna walk in there with your head held high like you own the place. You're gonna show them you're everything Landon wasn't."

That was ludicrous. "You can't be serious."

Wyatt started pulling her toward the house. "Marilyn Sofitel, I have never been more serious about anything in my life. And you know what we're going to do after church?"

"Curl up into a ball and die?" She was only half kidding.

He kept walking, tugging her along. "No, we're going to ride the carousel. Because I *will* get it working before I pick you up for church. And I am not taking no for an answer, so don't bother trying."

Chapter Fourteen

Half an hour later, Wyatt looked up into the high rafters of the building that housed the Wander Canyon Carousel. If he had a church, it might feel a bit like this room. If Wander was always watching, could it be such a stretch to think God was always watching, too? *Lord, if You are, now'd be a good time to show up and show off. This carousel has to work today. It has to.*

He tightened the final bolts and worked the chain into place over the teeth of the gears. He'd waved goodbye to Marilyn and the twins as they left the ranch and then headed straight here. This machine was going work if it was the last thing he did.

He was going to church service. He'd just said a prayer. He'd come to care for a woman more deeply than he ever thought possible. What was God up to here? *I'm so wrong for her. All this is so far out of my territory.* Church was at four—two hours from now—and he'd been at this for hours. He admitted the fact he'd been tamping down all morning: *I'm terrified.*

Wyatt was about to throw the lever that turned on

the carousel's lights when he heard the creak of the building's door pushing open. He looked up to find his father walking in. Dad looked as surprised to be here as Wyatt was to find him.

"How's it going?" Dad asked. "Got it working yet?"

"I think I may have got it this time. I was just about to throw the switch." He was sure Pauline would have said something about the perfect timing of Dad's appearance.

Dad walked farther into the room. "That was a fine thing you did this morning. Seeing to Marilyn Sofitel and her girls like you did."

Dad was so frugal with praise that his short statements felt monumental. Things had still been prickly between them since that morning months ago when he'd stormed off the ranch. It left Wyatt a bit stumped as to how to respond. "Um...thanks."

"Anything I can do to help?"

This was the closest thing to an olive branch Dad could offer. Wyatt felt almost sorry there wasn't anything to do but turn the carousel on and see if it finally worked. Could that be enough? "You want to throw the switch?"

If a single pair of questions could feel like reconciliation, this moment was the start. His father gave him a look that was a mix of apology, admiration and affection. Wyatt felt his breath hitch when Dad threw the power switch and the hundreds of tiny lights turned the space gold and glowing. Turning the lights on was only half the battle, however. The real triumph was in getting the carousel in motion. Wyatt pointed to the lever that engaged the finicky motor. "Go ahead and pull it."

For a moment there was a terrorizing silence, and then Wyatt heard the blissful thunk of the mechanism engaging. A series of clicks and whirrs heralded the machine parts launching into motion. Then, as if the whole carousel—maybe the whole canyon—were pulling in a breath, the platform began to move. A million mechanical stutters filled the air around him, and he turned away from the central column to watch in wonder as animals slowly began to parade by. The wheeze and hum of the calliope—a sound unlike any other, in his view—rose toward the first notes of the carousel's song.

"It works!"

"You fixed it," Dad said, grabbing his shoulder. "You fixed it."

The slow rotation of the platform and the rise-and-fall waves of animals felt as large as the solar system. When God's hand had set the planets in motion, it must have felt something like this.

Wyatt gave a whoop and stepped onto the moving platform as the carousel reached its full working speed and stayed there. It stayed there! He felt like vaulting himself onto the back of the eagle, kicking his legs out in celebration. Instead, he reached out a hand to his father, pulling him onto the platform as they went around together, just standing beside the moving animals and soaking in the victory. He, no-good Wyatt Walker, had restored the Wander Carousel to working order. He found himself glad his father was here to see the moment—something that astonished him.

Dad must have felt the same way. "I'm glad I got to see this," he said as the carousel finished its cycle and the music died down. It was the first genuine smile his father had given him in a long time. They'd made a cranky sort of peace for the family's sake, but right now felt like the first moment of real reconciliation.

"Me, too," Wyatt said, meaning it.

"I'm proud of you, son."

Wyatt hadn't realized how starved he was to hear those words until his father spoke them just now. Emotion tightened his throat and left him fumbling for a response. "Thanks," he managed, his voice thick.

They didn't quite know how to handle the moment. The carousel had stopped, and the silence amplified the awkwardness.

Dad finally stepped off the platform. "Well, I'll leave you to whatever else needs doing. And you should get cleaned up before church starts at four."

He was a greasy mess at the moment. Happy, but as grimy as his worst days at the garage. "I know."

He waited for his dad to launch into a speech about how long it had been since he'd had both his sons in pews at Wander Community Church, but Dad just offered a goofy grin and said, "See you soon."

"Yeah."

As the big red door pulled shut behind his father, Wyatt realized he was wearing a goofy grin himself. *I fixed the Wander Carousel.*

For no reason than his own enjoyment, Wyatt hit the lever to start up the mechanism again. When the music and motion began, he sat himself on the eagle for a victory lap. But he wasn't halfway around before he yanked his phone from his back pocket and dialed up Marilyn's number. He put the phone onto the speakerphone setting so it would catch the music. He didn't say anything as she answered, just let the calliope announce his victory.

"It's working?" her voice came over the clamor. "You fixed it?"

In the background he could hear a pair of delighted squeals that lodged in his heart. He'd be lying if he said he didn't take this on partly to play the hero—just once—for Wander Canyon. And it meant the world to him that his father had come and offered his pride. But this joyful noise, the triumph of this moving carousel, was really about only two people. Two little people who had somehow managed to cross the moat of disregard he'd built around himself. Tomorrow he'd shout to the entire canyon that he, no-good Wyatt Walker, had fixed the carousel. Tonight, after church, the only thing he wanted was to watch Margie and Maddie go around.

And see the joy on Marilyn's face when they did.

"I'll pick you up at three thirty. And this will be waiting for you after the service."

Wyatt could hear the smile in her voice when she said, "I can't wait."

As he pocketed the phone, still on the eagle as the carousel spun its way through the cycle, Wyatt caught sight of himself in one of the many mirrored panels that lined the ride's center pillar.

He looked ridiculous. A grown man grinning like an idiot atop a wildly painted eagle going up and down in mock flight. The furthest thing from the cool, collected, can't-touch-me face he showed the world. The face of the Carousel Man flashed back at him as it traveled across the mirrors. A strange new Wyatt. The reflection of someone who'd cracked open just enough to really care.

Was that okay? Was he looking at some matured, improved version of himself, or just the newest ploy for attention? Wyatt pointed at his reflection as it jumped from mirror to mirror, slowing down as the carousel did. "You don't even like kids," he said aloud to himself and the Carousel Man in the shiny gilded panels.

He didn't. Wyatt usually avoided children whenever possible. He was actually dreading the day Chaz and Yvonne would announce they were starting a family and he'd have to figure out how to be Uncle Wyatt. Mostly because he was so sure he'd be no better at that part of family life than he had been at being a son or a brother so far.

He'd gotten so used to messing things up with people that he'd stopped trying to get it right. Forgotten how good it felt to *get* it right. And this, he'd gotten right. The stubborn old machine was running right. He and his father had found their way to putting things right between them—at least that's how it felt. And before the sun went down today, he would lead Margie and Maddie through that door and put right that pair of pouts they'd worn when he first met them.

That was easy. It was the other part that had him scratching his head when the music finally gave way to silence. The Marilyn part.

He'd lost count of the number of dates he'd taken to this carousel, fully aware of how romantic women found it. It was a persuasion tactic, an easy penance for any of his many wrongdoings, not unlike the red cupcake tickets.

This was different.

Before he'd *used* the carousel. Tonight he'd be *giving* it. Not just to Margie and Maddie, but to Marilyn. And not just as the girls' mother. He wanted to lift Marilyn onto the ostrich she liked and stand right next to her as she threw her head back and laughed. He wanted to be the one to make her smile—and not just because the girls were smiling. He knew half a dozen ways to get a woman into his arms coming down off a carousel animal, but none of those schemes seemed worthy of Marilyn Sofitel.

A foreign thought hung in the air amid the gold glow of the carousel's many little lights. Women amused him, fascinated him, even distracted him, but he *admired* Marilyn. Who she was, how hard she fought to give the girls a good life, how she dared poke her nose into his business—literally into his business. Wyatt stood in front of the ostrich and pondered the strange notion. *What do I do with that? With her?*

Normally, Wyatt always knew what to do with women. It came second nature to him, and he was very good at it. Always had been. Kissing beautiful women was one of life's great pleasures in his view. He was very good at that, too.

Marilyn was neither his standard definition of beauty, nor his type. And while he gleefully ignored most standards of decency, he knew he would not ever kiss Marilyn in front of her girls.

But, to his great surprise, he couldn't say he didn't

want to. He *did* want to. Her? With him? Nothing made less sense in the world.

"She'd try to fix me," he lectured the ostrich's glossy wooden eye. "Those kinds always do." In fact, hadn't she already tried?

The trouble was, even he knew there was a difference between fix and help, and she'd genuinely tried to help him. And he needed it. He'd taken the section of the Sunday *Courier* with the harmful article about Landon from the table at the ranch and brought it with him to try to read it. The trouble he'd had getting through the exasperating paragraphs seemed to shout its own conviction. When he went to that session at the church learning center, Wyatt felt certain they'd confirm what Marilyn suspected. What she was brave enough to tell him even though he'd been a total jerk in his reaction.

He was grateful to her. He found her beautiful in ways he'd never considered before. He respected her and felt an honor in protecting her. And he was picking her up for church in a matter of hours.

Wyatt stared at the rafters again. *I could take this whole carousel apart and it wouldn't be as complicated as what I feel about her.*

Chapter Fifteen

Marilyn kept an iron grip on each girl's hand as they walked into the clearing behind Wander Canyon Community Church. Rows of folding chairs spread out in a peaceful semicircle around a picnic table pressed into service as an altar and pulpit. Under any other circumstances, she would find the scene pleasant. Iconic, even. At the moment, it looked more like a battlefield to her, the scene of a last stand.

"We never had church outside in Denver," Margie said to Wyatt as he walked beside them.

"That's too bad," he answered. "I think it beats the inside kind." She had to give Wyatt credit. He was managing to make this church appearance look perfectly ordinary even though Pauline had let it slip that this was Wyatt's first arrival at any service since Chaz and Yvonne's wedding. He was doing this for her, wielding his defiance on her behalf. Doing his best, even, to brashly draw attention to himself and away from her. There weren't words for how much that meant to her today.

They took their place beside Pauline and Hank Walker far too near the front of the chairs. "Sitting up front means they can't crane their necks around and stare," Wyatt had joked when she showed a wisp of apprehension. How did he do that? She didn't have his ability to slough off what other people thought. Marilyn prayed for some semblance of focus, that she wouldn't spend the next hour sensing people's stares as if they burned holes in her back.

She pulled in a deep breath and willed the warmth of the afternoon sunshine to send calm into her body. *Inhale. Exhale.* She made her list:

I'm thankful Maddie and Margie haven't really grasped what's happened.

I'm thankful for Pauline's kindness.

I'm thankful for Wyatt. That felt a bit dangerous to admit, even though it was so very true. He'd even chosen to sit on the aisle, placing himself physically between her family and anyone who might dare an unkind remark. With Pauline and Hank on her other side, she could almost convince herself she wasn't dangling out in the open like a target for hurtful gossip.

I need to feel like I can survive today. And the days to come.

I need to feel Your presence, Lord.

I need Your protection from hurtful words I can't withstand right now.

"I am sorry for all this," Pauline leaned over to whisper in Marilyn's ear, "but I won't say I'm sorry the Good Lord found a way to drag that boy back to church. Don't you doubt for a minute that He's got this, got Wyatt and got you." After a moment, she asked quietly, "Why aren't Ed and Katie here?"

"Gram and Gramps already went to the service inside this morning," Maddie piped up. The girls continued to be blissfully oblivious to the tensions of the grown-ups around them.

The look Marilyn exchanged with Pauline said it all. It was poignant, and telling, and more than a little sad that Mom and Dad made no offer to come with her and the girls to this outdoor service. In fact, Mom seemed rather put out that Marilyn would dare to show her face at all given the papers. *Oh, Mom, what you know now isn't even the half of it,* Marilyn wanted to yell.

Her parents' assumptions and expectations had been one of the things that made coming home so hard. Mom had considered Landon such a catch. She was endlessly proud of Marilyn's big house and fancy life in Denver. If Marilyn were honest, it sometimes bothered her how Mom spoke of Landon as if landing him was her daughter's greatest accomplishment. It chipped away at her sense of self, made it easier to swallow Landon's attitude of her worth coming solely through him. The pressure made it almost impossible to admit things hadn't come close to how they looked from the outside. As if she couldn't possibly reveal how far the truth had fallen from what everyone had thought.

A truth it felt like the whole world just discovered.

The tremble started back up her spine. *I'm not who I was.*

No. Wait. That's not true. A little shock of surprise went through her, halting the trembling. *I'm who I have always been. Your child, Lord. You haven't moved, You haven't changed. It's Landon who fell away, who became someone different.* Or, if what Wyatt said was true, had never been at all.

Oh, Father, forgive me. No wonder my faith has felt so shaky—I've been drawing my identity from all the wrong places.

It struck Marilyn at that moment that worship was exactly where she needed to be. And who would have guessed that Wyatt would have been the one to make it happen?

Despite Pauline's comforting words and even Wyatt's defiant position at the end of the aisle, Marilyn still felt like a feather, fragile and shaky. "Are we really going to the carousel after this?" Margie asked Wyatt for the tenth time. "You really got it to work?"

Wyatt somehow managed to give them a smile that was wide and welcome. As if nothing in the world had gone amiss this morning. "I did. And no one else gets to ride it before you and Maddie." It was nothing short of a wonder that he had, in fact, gotten the carousel working as he promised. Then again, the look he gave her before he left was absolute determination. That finicky piece of machinery had no choice but to bend to Wyatt's will today. He had somehow known it was the perfect gesture, the perfect prize at the end of what she could only hope to be a difficult hour enduring stares and whispers.

After a bit more chatter with the girls, Wyatt caught Marilyn's gaze above the girls' heads as the service was just about to start. "Okay so far?"

Even though she felt nowhere near okay, she forced a smile and said, "Okay."

He settled into the chair as if he'd been there for years. "Steady on." For a moment she had all but forgotten that his presence here was nearly as scandalous as she imagined hers to be.

"Hey there," Tessa's voice came from the pew behind her. "I got your back. Literally. We all do."

And there it was, God sending a friend to say just the words she needed to hear. She turned to see Tessa and three other moms from the Solos Bible study planted in the chairs just behind her. She really was surrounded by friends who would stand between her and wagging tongues.

Tessa put a warm hand on her shoulder. "I'm glad you showed up."

She managed a wisp of a smile. "Not as glad as I am that *you* showed up."

"Mr. Wyatt fixed the carousel," Margie said, her excitement making her whisper far too loud.

"Did he, now?" Tessa said. "That's some good news."

"You should put it in the paper," Maddie suggested, with no idea of the weight of such a remark given this morning's events.

"Good news is always worth printing, I'd say." Tessa gave Marilyn a wink. "We always need more good news."

"Welcome one and all," Pastor Newton announced as he called the congregation to the start of the service. "What a privilege it is to worship amid God's glory on such a beautiful day."

It *was* a beautiful day. She'd managed to miss that in all her strife and worry. *You still have beautiful days ahead waiting for me, Lord. Help me to remember that.*

Marilyn would have liked to say she paid close attention to the service, that she worshipped and sang with the focus it deserved, but that would have been a lie. She mostly survived the time. Each minute she didn't curl up into a ball felt like a tiny victory. No groundswell of community scorn swallowed her up. At Wyatt's suggestion, she kept her eyes front, not turning to look at the congregation behind her and give any chance for judgmental eyes to cast their shadows. Marilyn drew strength from Wyatt's presence on the other side of the girls. She allowed herself to feel the warmth of Pauline and Hank beside her, and from Tessa, Greg and the Solos sitting behind her.

As the final hymn was sung, Marilyn actually felt stronger. Less as if she'd blow away in the slightest wind. As He always had, God had met the three needs she'd asked of Him—well, two of them, anyway. She still couldn't guarantee that they'd make it out of the service and through the lemonade on the lawn afterward without hearing some barb.

In fact, that first barb arrived only minutes after the final note of the closing hymn. Norma Binton, a pinch-faced woman Marilyn vaguely remembered from the local drugstore counter, started walking toward her. Even Mom had little patience for Norma, and that was saying something.

"You ought to—"

Wyatt abruptly stepped between them. "—turn

right back around and go somewhere else," he finished in a tone that made his intention crystal clear.

Wyatt would could have guessed the first shot across the bow would come from Norma Binton. "Old Biddy Binton" they'd called her even back then, and the years hadn't mellowed her one bit.

"I'm not talking to you," she declared, craning her neck up and peering at him through her ever-present half-moon reading glasses that hung from a beaded chain around her neck. He was inappropriately glad for every inch of the full foot he had over the tiny woman. Her hair was pulled into a bun so tight they used to joke it cut off the circulation to her brain.

She started around him, nervy old bird that she was, but he stepped in her path again. "You're not talking to her, either."

"Excuse me?" she snapped.

"I said you're not talking to her, either, unless it's to say how *glad* you are to see her and her *adorable* girls in church today."

She blinked at him for a moment, startled, and then narrowed her eyes in determination.

Wyatt wasn't having it. "Or maybe how delighted you are to see me. It's been what—three years?" He spread his hands and raised his voice just enough to be heard by anyone nearby. "I'd think you be just tickled to see me back in church, Mrs. Binton. You are, aren't you?"

Her mouth shut so abruptly Wyatt heard her teeth clack together. God probably frowned on him enjoying baiting Old Biddy Binton as much as he did, but

Wyatt seemed to remember God having a soft spot for defending the weak. And Wyatt was certainly feeling up to the job of defending Marilyn and her girls this afternoon. *Make her back down, Lord,* he stunned himself by praying. *I might not do You proud if she picks a fight.*

God seemed to hear him, for Norma Binton turned on her sensible orthopedic heels and stalked off toward the table of baked goods without so much as another word.

Marilyn gave him a look that was so filled with relief Wyatt felt his stomach do a flip. Life didn't hand him many opportunities to play the hero—he'd forgotten what it could do to a guy. "Thanks." She practically exhaled the word.

"My pleasure," he said, meaning it. He shouldn't enjoy putting Norma Binton in her place like that. Especially not in church. But it made him feel ten feet tall for fending off whatever mean-spirited comment she was gearing up to launch at Marilyn. It had cost Mari a lot to show up today, to at least try to stand tall against what she was so sure was coming at her on account of Landon.

Marilyn wasn't entirely wrong. He'd lived in Wander long enough to know what small towns could do. He wouldn't be able to shield her from every mean comment, although he would sure try. He wanted to take her hand, or hold her again, but knew this wasn't the place. He wouldn't do anything to topple her unsteady composure, not here in front of too many eyes.

On their carousel ride later, however, he wasn't sure he could master such restraint. His hands itched with the feel of her fingers entwined in his, and the way her head lay against his chest when she cried by the stream felt burned in his memory.

Marilyn stared after the woman, now inside a knot of Wander women in deep conversation. "She won't be the last."

"Who knows? Maybe they will stay quiet." he replied, tamping down the urge to go declare his protection against the whole lot of them. They all never liked him anyway, so he had nothing to lose for Marilyn's sake.

The resignation in Marilyn's eyes made him want to go hit something. Why did the kindest people have to learn how mean life could be? "Okay, so not likely," he admitted. "So maybe we stay five more minutes just to show them you won't scare off, and then we make a break for the carousel. The way the girls are boasting, I won't be able to keep everyone else out much longer."

"And then you'll get to play hero," she said, her smile lighting a glow under his ribs. "Mr. Carousel Man."

I just did play hero, and it had nothing to do with that carousel. In truth, he took far more pride in fending off Norma Binton than in any community praise he might get for repairing the Wander Canyon Carousel. And that wasn't about any public reputation. It was about a personal involvement. About the crazy level of care he was coming to feel for Marilyn. And her girls. He'd have stayed up all night just to fix the carousel for the three of them and no one else.

And that scared him.

For the first time in his life, he felt the urge to be

careful with a woman. Careful. *Him*. He knew he had to tread carefully with her tender heart, to safeguard her wounded spirit. All this with the last woman on earth he would have pegged to throw him for this kind of loop. He'd just *gone to church for her*, for crying out loud.

"And you know how much I like playing hero," he said, dragging himself away from all such dangerous thoughts. He gave her a sly wink, a flash of his old self who would have enjoyed the double meaning of a man who never played hero. It didn't quite work, because for Marilyn he did like playing hero.

A pair of middle-aged couples Wyatt recognized as friends of Ed and Katie's started walking toward him and Marilyn. One of them had the nerve to be holding the newspaper with those headlines about Landon. They had a look he knew all too well on their faces. It was the polite but sharp look that always preceded words like "I don't mean to be unkind, but…"

He stepped in front of Marilyn and gave them his darkest "don't mess with me" glare. They slowed, but didn't stop.

He reached behind him and took Marilyn's elbow, guiding her in the other direction. "Yep, we're done here. Hey girls!" he called across the lawn. "Ready for that private carousel ride?"

His words had the intended effect, announcing to the crowd that the carousel was now working but that only Marilyn and the girls were allowed to ride for now. He was fully ready to declare, "I fixed it—who rides is my call," but folks were so startled that no one said a word. They all just stared as he and Marilyn gathered Margie and Maggie and headed toward the red carousel barn with something close to heads held high.

He'd let the rest of the town in when he was good and ready, but for right now he was going to lock that door tight behind them. He was going to give this family their own burst of happiness with no one around to ruin it.

Champion of defiance indeed.

Chapter Sixteen

As they walked the block and a half to the carousel building, Marilyn was grateful for the girls' nonstop excited chatter. It not only bathed her like an oil of grace, but it covered the growing pull between her and Wyatt. He was well on his way to winning her heart. With a carousel and a church service—who would have guessed? After all the stress and dread of the morning, she loved that the girls felt as if they'd been given a fabulous prize in this first ride.

"I'm so glad we helped you fix the ride!" Maggie said as they reached the bright red building. Marilyn's heart warmed with how they considered themselves helpers in Wyatt's accomplishments. He'd been so good to them. He'd been so good to her.

Wyatt unlocked the big red door and spread his arms wide in grinning triumph. It was such a small thing—this victory ride—and then again not small at all. In fact, it felt like the first big happy thing in far too long. "First things first." Wyatt hoisted a girl in each arm and raised them toward the sorry little Out of Order sign that had marked their first meeting.

"Yank it down, girls!" he commanded with mock authority.

With a whoop, the girls pulled down the sign and proceeded to cover Wyatt in hugs and giggles. She watched him try to stay coolly above all the affection, but the moment he gave in cracked her heart open. He squinted his eyes shut and hugged the girls back, head thrown back in an unguarded laughter she felt fill her own chest.

Wyatt caught her eyes as he lowered the girls to the ground, and the connection shot through Marilyn before she could stop it.

The girls dashed ahead into the building, and Wyatt held out his hand to her. "I got an ostrich in here with your name on it."

She couldn't have resisted for all the world. Suddenly a trip around that circle on a wooden ostrich called like the happiest thing in the world.

"Does it really work? You fixed it?" Maddie came back and began yanking Wyatt's arm toward the ride. Marilyn was grateful her exuberance broke the spell of Wyatt's eyes and the warmth of his hand on hers. She'd wanted this moment, even prayed the carousel would be fixed. But now that it was here, it felt wonderful and dangerous and weighty all at the same time.

"It really works," Wyatt boasted. "And now you get the first ride, just like I promised."

A pinch of shame rose in Marilyn's chest for having doubted him. The events of the past year had knocked too much out of her. Maybe today really could mark the return of the optimism she'd felt gone from her life. From her whole spirit. Wouldn't that be something?

Wyatt went into the center column to hit the power switch, illuminating the myriad golden twinkling lights. Then he came back out and stood in front of Maddie, dramatically scratching his head. "Wait, wait, don't tell me... I'll remember... You like the rooster."

"Yep!"

Wyatt scooped her up and trotted around the platform until, with great ceremony, he deposited her on the colorful bird.

"Safety first," he teased as he snapped the strap around her waist. She grinned, nearly bouncing on the rooster's wooden saddle in her delight.

He turned back to Margie, making the same show of searching his memory. "You like the seahorse, don't you?"

Maggie bobbed her head up and down in a happy nod. Marilyn found herself deeply touched by how he'd remembered.

"Up you go!" He set Maggie on the seahorse with great ceremony.

Marilyn suddenly realized she was next. Not at all ready to be lifted onto her mount by Wyatt, she tried to effect a casual run to the ostrich and jump on. It ended up instead looking like a goofy scramble, one she was sure broadcast her reluctance to let Wyatt get that close.

He, of course, was unfazed by the display. He strode over to her, holding her gaze for far too long, and then gently snapped the safety strap into place. How he made the simple act so dashing was beyond her. What his eyes did to her breath was beyond her, too. She found herself saying a quick flash of a thankful prayer that both girls' animals were within sight. He wouldn't try anything with the girls watching.

Worse yet, she wasn't actually sure what she would do if he did.

As if he'd read her mind, Wyatt winked at her. "Just relax and enjoy the ride," he said as he slowly turned and stepped back down toward the carousel's center pillar.

"Ladies," he said with all the showmanship of a circus ringmaster, "I give you the fully repaired Wander Canyon Carousel!" With that, he reached into the pillar and threw the lever that brought the ride to life.

Marilyn felt the mechanism whir to life, her ostrich rising on its pole as the calliope's happy notes filled the air. The girls' gleeful shouts and the dance of the lights against the walls felt like pure joy. She clung to the pole, welcoming how happy, dizzy and light she felt.

Wyatt seemed to move around the ride as if born to it, as if the lights and movement didn't faze him in the slightest. He stood over each of the two girls' rides, pointing things out and talking with them as if they were queens on golden chariots.

She held her breath as he strode around the arc of the platform, leaning in just a bit against the force of the spin. He stopped at the unicorn next to her, planting one foot into a stirrup and hanging on so that he rose and fell in counterbalance beside her. It placed him just close enough to let her feel his presence, but not so close that the hum of panic lingering just under her skin got the chance to take over.

"Thank you," he said, leaning toward her as they rose and fell in opposite waves. The dual movement was as exhilarating as it was unnerving. They were only two words, but his eyes said far more. Shouldn't she be thanking him?

He'd changed. The constant edge she'd seen in him, the defiance she'd always thought defined him, had softened. Marilyn was already off balance from the rotation of the ride, but it was Wyatt's eyes that truly made her grip the pole in front of her in order to hold steady. The man's eyes were breathtaking. Deep and rich and yet bright and gleaming. Filled with all the vibrancy she felt gone from her life.

Despite the storm still brewing outside these walls, Wyatt seemed to illuminate parts of her she'd consigned to darkness after Landon died. Even before Landon died. Life had been neat and tidy and…well, bland…for so long. Except for the girls, of course. They had always been the beacon pulling her onward, even in grief. Now life was messy and misdirected and confusing, but it felt like life again. Whirling around this glittering space, surrounded by music and laughter and whimsy, Marilyn felt possibilities open up before her. As if there really could be a happy ending despite what any paper chose to print. It was a startling, scary thing.

Something told her if the girls were not nearby, he might have kissed her. Her. The last person in the world to catch Wyatt Walker's attention. She was as sure of it as she was reluctant to believe it. Marilyn was grateful for the noise and movement, sure the dazzle of Wyatt's eyes would overwhelm her in silence.

He would have kissed her. She knew it. And she would have let him, even kissed him back. Worse yet, his eyes told her he knew what she was thinking.

Marilyn shut her eyes and gripped the carousel pole as if a hurricane was blowing through. Wasn't it? *Oh, Lord,* her heart yelped in prayer, *could this really lead anyplace safe?*

They ended up going through three cycles of the ride. Nobody wanted it to end. But as the carousel was slowing down the third time, Wyatt knew his resistance was failing. If he so much as took Marilyn's hand to help her off the ostrich, there'd be no going back. If he touched her even for a second, he would kiss her. Whether it made sense or not, whether the girls were watching or not. And for once in his life he was going to show a little restraint. Make that a whole lot of restraint.

"Okay, little ladies, all done here. Time to get you back home." The words out of his mouth sounded so *responsible.* What was happening to him?

The twins whined and pouted as he unbuckled them and lifted them from their mounts. "Aw, do we hafta?"

"I think we've taken up enough of Mr. Wyatt's time today," Marilyn said as she slipped down from the ostrich.

That wasn't true. He had all the time in the world for Marilyn and her daughters. He couldn't stop thinking about her or the girls. A mom with two kids—how had *that* happened? He couldn't figure out how she'd managed to poke her way into his world. She had toppled things he didn't know how to put back in order. It felt like a tornado had blown through his life.

Not the least of it was the dyslexia thing. Oh, sure, he'd denied it at first, but he knew she was right. Marilyn had offered an explanation to something that had chased him all his life, and it had sent everything askew. Including his heart. The whole thing was beyond irrational, beyond understanding, and worst of all, beyond his control.

As he locked up the building and they turned to walk toward where the car was still parked at the church, Wyatt felt Marilyn's hand slide into his. The simple gesture took his breath away. What was the word Dad always used when he talked about how hard he fell for Pauline? *Thunderstruck.* He understood now how Dad and Chaz talked about the loves in their lives now.

Love? *Love?* It made him crazy how the words seemed to fit what he was feeling.

There was only one problem—and it was a whopping one. Wyatt knew he was the last person on earth who could give them what they really needed. No dyslexia clouded his ability to see that. Fun was his thing. Commitment and stability were not. Even if he gave in to what he was feeling, it would surely burn out fast. He'd fail them sooner or later, walk away the way he always did when things got tough. They deserved so much better than that.

The smart move would be to run in the other direction, right now. But he couldn't. Even as he loaded the girls onto their booster seats in the backseat of his pickup—there were booster seats in the backseat of his pickup truck!—he knew he was powerless to cut them out of his life.

They reached the Ralton house far too soon. The girls piled out of the car and rushed up to the front door, where Grandma stood waiting. He heard them gush about riding the carousel, but it was mostly noise behind the roar of his own heart and the look in Marilyn's eyes.

"Thank you for today," Marilyn said, her expression

telling him what he already knew. There were a million things they needed to say to each other, and all of them would have to wait. "For everything. I don't... I don't know how I could have gotten through today without you."

"I was glad to do it," he said as he pulled the booster seats out of his truck and set them on the front sidewalk. He was glad to do it, but glad was so far from the full power of what he was feeling.

"Mari," Katie said with an unmistakable insistence. "Supper's almost ready."

He cracked a smile as Mari walked him back to the truck. "I think I hear your mother calling," he joked as he got into the vehicle just to keep the safety of the door between them.

She laughed. He wanted to capture her laugh and tuck it away someplace. Nothing had ever made him feel like he did when she laughed.

Marilyn sighed and bit her bottom lip, resting her hands just inside the truck's open window. "Wyatt..."

If she said his name like that one more time, he'd lean out the window and kiss her no matter what the consequences. Wyatt put his hand on top of hers. "G'night." Dumb, but he couldn't think clearly enough to come up with something better to say.

"Good night, Wyatt."

It took everything he had to put the truck in gear and pull it out of the driveway. The ride home was too silent. The garage was too empty as well when he got there, and his apartment felt blisteringly silent when he opened the door. He was pretty sure the silence and his heart would haunt him all night, and they did.

Chapter Seventeen

Ron Camden pulled a rusty truck into the garage bay late Monday morning. The engine knocked and rattled as it shut down, the door giving a mighty squeak as Ron climbed out of the cab.

"I can't believe you've kept that thing running," Wyatt said. If a vehicle could look as if it were gasping its last breath, this one did. He'd been hopelessly distracted all morning. Maybe this problematic truck would force his attention back to his work.

"Now I gotta," Ron said. "Can you give me a hand to keep it going one more year?"

"Always did like a challenge," Wyatt offered. "You like her that much?" He suspected Ron just didn't have the funds to replace it, but didn't want to say as much.

Ron gave the truck a scowl. "I'm growing to hate her, actually. But we're gonna have to stick with each other one more year now."

That was telling. Ron was one of the struggling ranchers sitting on an offer from Mountain Vista. "How so?"

"I've decided not to take the Mountain Vista offer. It isn't what the land is worth, and after yesterday I'm not so keen on how they do business over there."

You and me both, Wyatt thought to himself. "If you ever do sell, it should be for a good price. And to somebody you feel good about."

"Nice thought," Ron agreed. "A bit harder to make happen, though. It's gonna be tight."

It took Wyatt only a second to decide. "How about I give you half off labor to support the cause?"

"You'd do that?"

This hero thing was growing on him. "Sure I would." Manny would back him up, he had no doubt.

"Well, if you can get the carousel up and running, I'm sure you can do whatever it takes to squeeze another year out of this scrap heap."

Word of the carousel working again had flown through town. It hadn't completely drowned out gossip about Landon Sofitel, but it had made a satisfying dent. And it had been fun to call the Carousel Committee chair and tell her to send the volunteer ticket-takers back to work. Every once in a while all morning he would stop work and listen for the faint and gratifying sound of calliope music echoing across the canyon.

"Let's hope so." Wyatt swept his eyes over the vehicle, making a mental list of what might need to be done. "Give me forty-five minutes and I'll have a workup for you." A new amusing thought hit him. "You like chocolate, Ron?"

"Who doesn't?"

He reached into his pocket to extract one of his red tickets. He'd never given one to a male before, but why not change this along with everything else? Wyatt felt a smirk creep across his face. "Head down to the Wander Bakery. My sister-in-law, Yvonne, will serve you up a cup of coffee and one of her brownies while I get you squared away. My treat." He chuckled at the idea of how Yvonne's eyes would pop at one of his freebie tickets turning up in the hands of an old man. Heroism was turning out to be more fun than he thought.

Rob smiled. "Well, that's kind of you." After a pause, he added, "Guess church must've done you good."

Wyatt felt his face flush. "Oh, I don't know about that."

"Don't think I didn't see you follow that lady into church yesterday afternoon. I always told Janice it would be a pretty face that lured you back into the fold." He chuckled. "Didn't count on three of 'em."

Marilyn didn't need to be the subject of more speculation. "Look, Ron, it's not—"

Ron held up a hand. "Sure it is. And not a thing wrong with it." He leaned in with a sparkle in his eye. "Have you told her?"

Wyatt calculated the odds of successfully denying it. The way he felt this morning, he didn't seem to stand much of a chance. Feeling absurdly sheepish, he muttered, "Um...no."

This seemed to tickle Ron even more. "She knows," he said with a conspiratorial wink.

"Huh?"

"She knows. It was all over her face. You saw it, right?"

It suddenly struck Wyatt that Sunday afternoon

was now proving to be one of the first times in recent memory he was too worried about what everyone else was thinking to further his own agenda. He'd been too focused on fending off anyone's mean comments to even notice what Marilyn was thinking.

Of course, that hadn't been the case at all at the carousel. He'd seen the way she looked at him, the cautious yearning in her eyes. He'd felt the world shift a bit when she slipped her hand into his, the way she stopped herself from leaning closer to him through the truck window. The old Wyatt wouldn't have hesitated to capitalize on that. Only he had somehow became a different man around Marilyn. One who actually stopped himself from taking advantage.

One who went to church in order to keep her safe.

One who couldn't get the giggles of two little girls out of his head.

"Yeah," he replied, the admission feeling huge, "I suppose I did."

Ron bumped his shoulder as if they were schoolboys. "Woman like her could do a lot worse than a man like you." With that endorsement and a gleeful wave, Ron headed out the door toward his coffee and brownie. "You think about that. And I'll see you later."

Wyatt shook his head and popped the hood of the rusty old truck. He'd go twice the extra mile now to help Ron make it last for another year. Maybe even throw in a replacement battery, no charge.

He scanned the engine and all the other parts, taking stock the way he always did. "Just stare at her for a while," Manny always said of any vehicle, "and she'll tell you what she needs."

He stared at the metal, tubes and gears, but didn't see an engine. He kept seeing Marilyn's face in the unguarded moments where she looked—really looked—at him. Those amazing seconds before her constant caution pulled her back. The moments where he felt himself short of breath and off balance. Thunderstruck.

Marilyn's face did tell him what she needed. She needed love, and constancy, and loyalty. A man of faith, devotion and rock-solid dependability.

Trouble was, he couldn't be at all sure that meant she needed *him*. But maybe it was time to try.

Marilyn squinted out her bedroom window Monday afternoon to see if she really was seeing what she thought she saw. There, at the end of the long drive, sat Wyatt's truck. And Wyatt, pacing up and down the fencing as if he couldn't decide whether or not to step onto the property. Even from this distance, she could see it in his body language: he was as undone by what was happening between them as she was.

The girls were in the back putting together birdhouse kits Dad had bought them at the hardware store. Marilyn walked downstairs to find Mom settled in her favorite chair with a book in her lap. She was staring out the living room window at the same sight Marilyn could see from her bedroom.

"Who is that at the end of the drive?"

Marilyn thought about dodging the subject, but decided against it. "Wyatt Walker," she said, making sure there was no tone of apology in her voice.

"What on earth is he doing here?" Mom's voice was filled with disapproval.

"I expect he wants to talk to me. So I'm going to walk out there and talk to him."

To her surprise, the look Mom gave her had no effect. She'd come to a turning point with her mother, one that was long overdue. It felt as if she crossed a lot more than property lines as Marilyn walked down the long drive toward Wyatt.

She could see the moment he saw her coming. The set of his shoulders changed, he stopped pacing. After a moment, he started walking toward her. The urgency she felt seemed to quicken his steps, as well.

"You're here," she said when they were close enough to speak. It seemed a ridiculous thing to say, but his presence did say a great many things.

"I couldn't stay away." He shifted his weight. "I... I don't know how to do this. I'm not even sure I can do this." He looked into her eyes. "But you...the girls... I want to try. I mean, it's not just me, right? You feel it?" He reached for her hand.

She gave it to him freely, easily. The overwhelming glowing sensation in her chest didn't really surprise her. Could a heart coming back to life feel any other way? "Are you asking if I care about you?"

He looked scared. More unsure of himself than she'd ever seen him. Funny how that made him even more handsome. "Not really," he said.

The answer unnerved her until he pulled her closer with the hand he held in his. "I think what I'm asking is if you love me. Because, well, I love you. And despite all the reasons we shouldn't be together, I'm really, really hoping I'm not alone in this."

For a man with such a legendary reputation as a

charmer, it was the most bumbling declaration of love she'd ever heard. It charmed her beyond reason. She stepped right up to him so that they were mere inches apart. He looked relieved, jubilant even. "No, Wyatt, you aren't alone in this. I do love you. The girls love you. Those are the best reasons—maybe the *only* reasons—to be together. And I don't know how this all works, either. But I want to try."

His smile was dazzling as he touched her cheek. It was as if her whole being bloomed back into life. The future changed from a test of endurance to a marvelous unfolding adventure. "Margie, Maddie... It's like I can't imagine living without them." He wrapped his arms around her. "Or you." His forehead touched hers. "I really hope your mom isn't watching because I'm about to kiss the daylights out of you."

She laughed and tilted her head toward his. "She is. Kiss me anyway."

Wyatt's kiss was everything. It was tender and warm and full of astonishment. Marilyn wondered if it could possibly feel as *never-been-anything-like-it* for him as it did for her. His touch filled her with new life and long-forgotten hope. And when he pulled back to look in her eyes, his eyes lit with the marvel that made her own chest glow.

"So that's what it's like to kiss the woman you love." He said it with the most endearing surprise. "Who knew what I was missing?"

"Who knew?" Marilyn said, smiling wide. She knew. She knew she'd found what she'd been missing. Hope, love, and the heart of a truly good man.

Chapter Eighteen

❧

Wednesday was Manny's first official day back at the garage, and Wyatt was near useless. He'd have to take back all those times he gave Dad grief for being a total mess after falling for Pauline. Love seemed to make a man temporarily stupid. Good thing Manny was back on the job as of today. He was itching to tell Manny about Marilyn, to get the wise old man's take on all the ways his life had turned upside down in recent weeks.

Only when Manny arrived, he looked just plain run-down. He puttered aimlessly around the shop if the last thing he wanted to do was work. He'd always thought of Manny like Dad—both men didn't know how to not work. Getting things done was like breathing, how they stayed alive.

"How's Peggy today?" Wyatt called out casually as he applied a grease gun to an axle.

"You already asked me that," came Manny's reply from under a sedan, followed by the clang of something dropping and a grumble of frustration.

"You okay?"

"When are you gonna stop playing mother hen and finish that brake job?"

Wyatt capped the grease gun. "I am done, you old coot. What'd you drop?"

"My standards when I hired you." Manny's creaky laugh echoed out from under the vehicle.

"As if you could make it without me." They had some version of this teasing exchange nearly every day since Wyatt had started helping out at the garage. It was mostly joking, but the thread of truth as to how much they enjoyed and counted on each other simmered underneath the humor.

Manny slid into view and sat up. "About that…" Wyatt did not care for the slow, grunting effort the man had to put in righting himself.

"What about it?"

"I been thinking…"

That could mean only one thing. A little burst of panic lit in Wyatt's gut, popping the bubble of bliss he'd been walking around in since kissing Marilyn. *Now? Really?* He'd been dreading the day Manny opted to close up shop. Even if he learned every clever tactic the learning center could offer, he was far from being able to go out into business on his own. He certainly had no desire to work for one of the snazzy car dealerships in the next town, Mountain Vista was definitely off the table and, while he and Dad had patched things up, that didn't mean he would go back to the ranch. He hated the idea of drifting again, especially with Marilyn and the girls in the picture.

Manny walked over to his desk, motioning for

Wyatt to follow. "Did you know I opened this place in 1964? This building wasn't even here. Just a garage shed and my toolbox."

This sounded too much like a goodbye speech. "I know that."

"I wasn't sure I could pull it off. Not back then, and not for a couple a years after that. But I stuck with it." Manny gave Wyatt a serious look. "Some things are worth sticking with."

That was rather a peculiar statement, seeing as Manny took Wyatt in when he did the exact opposite of sticking with Wander Canyon Ranch. Back then Manny was the only person who understood why Wyatt had walked away from the family herd and property. "I appreciate the way you stuck with me, Manny." A surge of sentiment tightened Wyatt's throat. "It's been a good run."

Manny leaned back in his chair. "Now, what makes you think that run is over?"

"'Cause this sounds a lot like an 'I'm retiring' speech, that's why."

"I am retiring."

He fully deserved to, but the three words still felt like the finale of some of the best months of Wyatt's life. He'd loved it here. He'd found himself, become his own person. He'd met Marilyn here, fallen for her and the girls as they spent time here. "I'll be sorry to see this place go." It was easy to admit that. These bays and the apartment above were home to him. More home, oddly enough, than he'd felt in his last five years at his childhood home of Wander Canyon Ranch.

"Who says it's going?"

Of course Manny wouldn't just close down the garage. He'd sell it. He'd built up a solid business. More than once Wyatt had daydreamed about swallowing his pride and asking Dad to loan him the money to make Manny an offer. He supposed he could strike a deal with the new owner, but did it stand any chance of being like working for Manny? "Isn't it?"

Manny chuckled. "I thought you were quicker on the uptake, boy."

Wyatt leaned back against the work counter and crossed his arms over his chest. "How about you just come clean with me about who's buying the place?"

Manny's chuckle broke open into a laugh. "*You* are."

That actually stung. "I can't." He'd give anything to swing purchasing this place, but it'd be years from now. He wasn't near ready to, financially or organizationally—he'd need a dozen Marilyns to pull that off.

"Well, not yet, no."

"You're not making any sense, old man."

"You're gonna buy it from me bit by bit. Much as you can, fast or slow as you can manage it." He straightened up. "You didn't actually think I'd up and sell this place to anyone else, did you?"

Did he hear that right? "Wait… Me?"

"It's called financing. As in me financing you. Instead of me paying you, you run this place and pay me for ownership. Ease into it. Best of both worlds. I just come in, say, once a week. Peggy says she's not keen to have me home bugging her all the time anyhow."

Wyatt felt like he had to be extra sure he'd heard what he thought he had. "You're gonna let me buy the business from you in payments?"

"That's what I just said, isn't it?"

"Um…yeah."

Manny's expression was an amused sort of puzzled. "You do want to run the garage, don't you?"

"Yes," Wyatt answered without hesitation. "Absolutely."

"Honestly, I half expected you to come to me with the idea. Carl at the bank brought it up the other week. I figured you were just being nice, waiting until Peggy and I were ready."

Wyatt wiped his hands on a rag, happily stunned. "Am I ready?"

"Well, maybe not on your own, but seems to me you might have the right sort of partner within reach now." Wyatt raised an eyebrow. "You shoulda heard Katie Ralton complaining to her lady friends in the diner this morning about 'that no-good Wyatt Walker' kissing her daughter at the end of her driveway." He laughed so hard he wheezed a bit. "Wander's always watching, isn't that what you say?"

Wyatt practically gulped. "So everybody knows?"

"If they don't, they will. She's yours now. That is unless you're dumb enough to let her get away." After a pause, he added, "You're not that dumb, are you?"

Chaz had told him once about the moment he saw his future line up bright and shiny in front of him. As if the storm ahead of him in life had burned off the way storms so often did in this part of the country. After a tumultuous season, and even a fistfight with Wyatt himself, Chaz had struggled through to making a future for himself and Yvonne on Wander Canyon Ranch. Now Wyatt felt he was standing on the same brink of a future he'd never thought possible. "No, Manny," he heard himself saying. "I'm not that dumb. I can't let her get away."

Manny grinned. "Now there ya go."

Wyatt had never been a patient man. Suddenly his impatience to step into that bright future practically swallowed him whole. He didn't want to wait one hour more to reach for what life—no, what God— had spread out before him. *Thanks for Your infinite patience with me, Lord. I expect I sorely tested You.* Wyatt checked his watch. Marilyn should be getting out of her meeting with Gail at the Chamber of Commerce just about now. The girls were still at the craft day they talked about at Sunday's church service. "You think you can hold this place down on your own for an hour or two, old man?"

Manny's grin widened. "Been doing it for years before you got here."

"I got something I gotta do."

"I expect you do." Manny surprised Wyatt by standing up and pulling him into a hug. "Go get 'er."

"I plan to. All three of 'em."

Gail slid the paper across the desk toward Marilyn. "So, here's what we're prepared to offer you. It's probably way below what you were used to in Denver, but we're a small operation here."

Marilyn wondered if it was professionally appropriate to look aghast. She hoped so, because she had no hope of hiding it. "You told me you weren't expanding here at the chamber."

Gail blushed. "Well, that's before we found out *I*

was expanding." When Marilyn gave her a quizzical look, Gail laid her hand on her belly. "I'm due in January."

"You're expecting!" Marilyn cried out.

"Expecting, expanding, and...exhausted. We'd be essentially job-sharing. Are you okay with that?"

"Absolutely!" The hours and salary fit Marilyn's needs perfectly. Still, she felt she had to ask. "You're okay with...me?" After all, this was a public relations position representing Wander Canyon, and there were still going to be people who stared a bit too long or wouldn't quite meet her eyes.

Gail gave her an understanding look. "I can't think of anyone better for the job. And quite frankly, I think the world doesn't have a better set of problem-solvers than a pair of working mothers."

Marilyn laughed. "You're right there." There had been a time when the threat of looks and questions would have kept her in hiding. She was on her way to becoming a different woman now. Wyatt had peeled away the layers of need and doubt that Landon had created. She knew, now, that she would never allow someone to do that to her again. She could—and would—teach her girls the same strength and sense of self.

A gush of gratitude filled her, as if the tight knot that had been in her stomach for months finally eased its grip.

They talked for a few more minutes about schedules and logistics. By the end of the conversation, Marilyn had no doubt the job would be a perfect fit. At one point, she looked out the office window to one side and caught sight of an anxious-looking Wyatt pacing the sidewalk in front of the building.

Gail gave a knowing smile. "I think someone is impatient to see you." She handed a folder to Marilyn. "Here's a draft of the fall and winter schedule and a list of the regular meetings. Can you start next Monday?"

Marilyn thought how good it would feel to have a place to use her talents, to feel truly part of the community. "I could start tomorrow."

Gail laughed. "Next Monday will be fine."

Marilyn calmly gathered her things, keeping mostly professional until she made it out of the office door. At that point, she rushed at Wyatt with a glee fit for Margie and Maddie. "Good news!" she called to Wyatt. He wrapped her in a hug without the slightest hesitation. Wyatt's embraces were like the man—strong and dramatic and enthralling. He had shown her just how pale and halfhearted her life had become. And now he was showing her how bright and bold it could be.

"Me, too," he said, squeezing her hands as he gave her a kiss. On the lips. Landon had a policy—and how telling it was that her mind used that word—of kissing her only on the cheek in public. Wyatt kissed her as if the whole world should know how deeply he felt about her. As if Wander could watch all they wanted. There was something warm and wonderful about that.

"You first," Wyatt said as he pulled back.

Landon always declared his news before hers. Her world was changing in so many ways.

"Gail offered me a position! Job-sharing with her. She's expecting and they need someone to divide the workload and take over for her when she's on leave. The hours are perfect. Everything's perfect."

"That's amazing!" His eyes told her he was genuinely happy for her. "You'll be fabulous at it."

She felt almost breathless with happiness, wondering just how much more joy the world could hold for her. "What's your good news?"

Wyatt stepped back and spread his hands. "You are looking at the new partner and future owner of a certain highly successful auto garage."

That was fabulous news indeed. "Really?"

"I thought Manny was telling me he was selling the place. But he wants to sell to *me*. A sort of pay-as-you-go setup that allows him to scale back and eventually retire." He grinned. "I'm gonna own the garage." He pulled her close again. "I feel like the king of the world."

"A promotion above the Carousel Man?"

"I'm thinking I just may keep that title. I mean, these days I feel like I've got enough fabulousness to spread around." It was all joy, no boasting. No positioning, no tactics. She'd been part of a network in Denver, but this is what it felt like to be part of a community. How had she allowed herself to forget that?

His eyes grew serious for a moment. "Everybody knows."

"Maybe they're as amazed that we fell in love as we are. Do you care?"

"Nope. Do you?"

She surprised herself by answering, "Not a bit. Our friends know what a good thing this is. The rest will just have to figure it out." It felt wonderful to remember she had good friends here.

Wyatt took her face gently in his hands. "What about the girls—are they okay?" As if it still baffled him, he added, "Do you have any idea how much I love your girls?"

Those were the only words that could fill her heart more than it already was. Speech left her, and she managed a nod as she felt a happy tear slide down one cheek.

Wyatt wiped it away with his thumb. "I love you. All of Wander could raise a monumental stink about it and I'd still love you." Way back then, she'd known a Wyatt who was brazen, defiant and mesmerizing. The man holding her in her arms was still a bit of those things, but he had also grown into a man who was loyal, true to himself and those he cared about, and strong. A man she could love without fear or doubt.

Wander Canyon had blue skies and bright sunshine most days of the year. But today the skies were far bluer, the sun far brighter, and the world opened up to new possibilities Marilyn had doubted would ever come.

A delightful version of her traditional list sparkled in her mind:

Three things I'm thankful for:
1. Wyatt.
2. Wyatt.
3. Wyatt.
Three things I need:
1. Wyatt.
2. Wyatt.
3. Wyatt.

Chapter Nineteen

Wyatt knew he had about fifteen minutes to execute his vital mission. He herded the girls into the carousel building, now surrounded by pumpkins and all manner of fall decorations. His nerves made his steps so fast Maddie and Margie had to almost run to catch up to him.

"I want the sheep today!" Margie cried out, the pair of them starting their dash toward the animals.

He caught them just in time. "Hang on. We can't ride just yet. We've got to do something first."

Maddie looked annoyed. "What?" He was pretty sure their pouting would dissolve once he revealed his plans.

"I have a super-important question to ask you, and then I'm gonna need my helpers to give me a hand on a really important choice." He motioned for them to sit on the edge of the carousel platform, one on each side of him.

Margie sat right down, hands hugging her knees. "Okay."

He took a deep breath and dived in. "You know I've been spending a lot of time with your mom. That's because I really like her."

Maddie shifted toward him and pinned him with one of her matter-of-fact stares. "No, you don't."

That wasn't how he planned on this going. "Huh?"

"You love her. That's not the same as like. And she loves you. She told us."

"Love's way better than like." Margie said it as if it were the simplest thing in the world, rather than the stunning truth that had knocked him off his feet in recent months.

He felt surrounded in more ways than one. "It sure is." He stretched out his arms, one around each of the girl's shoulders. It felt so incredibly perfect. Like something he'd feel proud to do for the rest of his life. "So lots of times, when people love each other, they get married. I was wondering how you'd feel about me marrying your mom."

Margie squished her face up in thought. "Would you be our dad?"

Wyatt had given a lot of thought as to how to phrase this. "Well, now, I know you already have one of those, and just because he's in heaven doesn't mean he stops being your dad. I'd be your stepdad, which is a different kind of dad who loves you just as much." It stunned him how much his voice hitched on the declaration of love for the girls. He did love them. Enormously. So much more than he would have ever thought possible.

"Aren't you supposed to ask *her*?" That was 100 percent Maddie. Straight to the point.

He pulled his arm from the girl to reach into his

pocket. "Well, I'm gonna when she gets here. But I figured I had to get your okay first." He opened the small blue velvet pouch that held the diamond ring Dad had given Mom. Yvonne now wore the one Dad had given Chaz's mom, and it seemed to form a perfect circle that Marilyn would wear the one his mother wore. If she said yes, that is. "What do you think?"

Margie was the first to grant her approval. "It's bee-u-tee-ful and she's gonna say yes."

"You think so?" Wyatt asked, almost embarrassed at how relieved he was to hear it.

"Yep," chimed in Maddie, as if it were as easy as choosing an ice cream flavor. Maybe it was. He couldn't hope to say—he'd never been in love before. He'd certainly never proposed before—on a carousel or otherwise.

"So you both are okay with this?" Love had reduced him to needing confirmation from first-graders. Granted, they were the most important first-grade girls on the planet to him, but he had a feeling God was enjoying stretching him in these strange new ways.

Margie decided to press the point. "So are you in love with us, too?"

It didn't take him even a second to answer. "You betcha." He pulled them into a great big three-person hug that nearly sent them tumbling back on the carousel platform. "But no telling until I ask your mom. We gotta surprise her. Which is why I need your help."

"Sure!" Maggie said, still giggling.

"Some carousels have a brass ring you try to grab for a special prize. I'm going to set that up for your mom. Normally, you have to try to grab it while you ride by, but I want to make extra sure your mom gets it. You've already seen the prize, but I have to decide which animal to put it on. Can you help me choose?"

"The ostrich is her favorite."

He'd already thought of that. "The ostrich was her old favorite. I want us to pick her a new one for our new life together." It sounded cheesy, but that's really how he felt. The ostrich spoke too much of the old Marilyn. He started walking around the carousel. "We have to get this exactly right."

"We do," agreed Maddie, taking the choice very seriously. She stopped on her trip around the carousel and turned to look back at Wyatt with almost somber eyes. "It's gotta be the swan."

He and Margie thought about it for a moment, and suddenly there was no other choice than the elegant white bird with the stretched-out neck and grandly spread wings. "Gotta be," he agreed, walking over to tie the blue pouch at just the right spot on the pole above the swan. He could stand on the front of it, rising and falling with Marilyn as she rode, facing her as he asked her to spend the rest of her life by his side.

"We'll ride these two," Maddie said, pointing to the turtle and the owl just behind the swan. "We won't look when you kiss her."

Wyatt could only laugh. If Marilyn said yes, he'd kiss her in front of all of Colorado and not care who watched. "She'll be here any minute." He gave his shoulders a shake. "I'm nervous." Why on earth was he admitting that to the girls?

"Why?" Margie said with complete innocence.

"She's gonna say yes. Gramps says she's broomed off her shoes."

It took Wyatt a minute to work it out. "Your grandfather thinks I've swept her off her feet?"

"Yep. That's it."

He didn't know if he'd won over Katie Ralton yet, but it sounded like Ed Ralton was in his corner. He'd take that victory.

Wyatt checked his watch and tried to stand casually by the carousel as if his heart wasn't pounding in his throat. The pounding was replaced by a huge lump as Margie and Maddie each took one of his hands and they waited together.

Come on, Lord, Wyatt prayed as he watched for Marilyn to come through the door. *You've done some pretty impossible things so far. Let's just shoot for one more.*

Marilyn walked into the carousel house with a smile on her face. She smiled so often now. Funny how you forgot how that changed things. She'd felt the welcome shift in her spirit from survival to hope, thankful she could pass that vital hope on to her daughters. Growing up in Wander, the carousel had always meant joy to her. Now it meant so many more things.

"Mom!" Margie and Maddie ran up to her, offering extra-enthusiastic hugs this afternoon. Wyatt seemed to have that effect on the girls, filling them with the same zest for life that drew her to him. "We've been waiting for you!"

Wyatt stood by the carousel platform. He looked distracted, but then again the girls were masters of distraction. She always marveled that for a man who never had been a parent, he seemed to have endless ways of involving the girls in every aspect of his life. He had the oddest expression on his face as he hopped up onto the platform and made his way toward the switch that would set the ride in motion. "Hop on, ladies."

They always rode when they visited Wyatt. Even if the carousel wasn't officially open—which it wasn't due to be for another thirty minutes—he turned it on for a private ride. It was a small thing, but it made the girls feel so special. Silly as it was, it made her feel special, too. She often found herself humming the calliope songs, smiling at all the memories.

Instead of heading for their usual favorite animals, the girls went straight to a pair on the other side of the platform. And when she turned toward the ostrich, Wyatt's hand gently pulled her away.

"You gotta ride this one today." Maddie pointed with amusing seriousness toward the swan in the row just in front of them.

Something was up. Conspiratorial looks passed between Wyatt and the girls as he checked their harnesses, pulled the lever to set the ride in motion and directed Marilyn toward the swan.

"Okay, then." When she glanced at him for an explanation as the platform began to move, he merely shrugged. When he helped her up onto the graceful white bird, the glint in his eye turned to something else. Nervousness.

As the swan began its slow arc of up and down, he stepped up on its wooden feet so that he rose up and down with her, facing her. It was both grounding and dizzying to travel around the circle with him in front of her like that. He placed one hand over hers on the pole as she held it, and she was reminded again how the warmth of his hands always held such comfort for her.

"Back in the day some carousels would mount a brass ring on the outside rim of the ride just barely within reach. The idea was to try to grab it as you went by, but it was tricky. Older carousels didn't have animals that moved on the outer rows, so they got ignored. Someone came up with the ring game to fix that. It's where the expression 'grab the brass ring' came from."

"I've heard the expression, but why the history lesson?"

"Well, you know me. I'm not much for playing by the rules. So I switched them up a bit." He pointed up with his free hand.

She followed his gesture, eyes looking up the pole until she saw a small blue pouch tied a few feet above her head.

"Your turn to grab the ring," he said. "Easy as pie."

She had to rise up a bit off the swan to reach it, and she felt Wyatt's hands reach around the pole to steady her. It was a marvelous little picture of their relationship—her reaching for a prize while he steadied her and the girls looked on. The ribbon holding the pouch pulled out of its knot easily, releasing the small velvet bag to fall into her hands. As she sat back down, Wyatt took the bag out of her palm and reached inside.

The lights, the music, the movement, all of it mixed with the dazzle in Wyatt's eyes as he held up the delicate gold ring with its simple square diamond. "You're my ring, Mari. My prize. I could take on the whole world if I knew you'd be beside me. Will you marry me?"

There wasn't a better reason in the whole world to be dizzy. "Yes," she said without a moment's hesitation or the tiniest shred of doubt. And while she wouldn't have thought a long, sweet kiss on a moving carousel swan to be possible, it most certainly was.

"You're gonna be Mrs. Carousel Man!" Margie cheered from her mount behind them.

Marilyn laughed. "Well, I hadn't thought about it that way, but I suppose that's true."

"I guess that makes you the Carousel Twins," Wyatt said. Marilyn loved the joy that filled his voice.

Margie looked at her sister. "The Carousel Twins!" Together, in time with the music, they began to sing their new titles over and over.

Wyatt kissed her again. When the ride and the song drew to a close, he helped her off the gorgeous wooden swan. "Why this one?" she thought to ask.

"The girls chose it. I told them it was time to leave the ostrich behind and asked them to pick you a new favorite. I think they did pretty good."

How perfectly wonderful of him to find a way to include the girls in his proposal. "Do you have any idea what an amazing parent you're going to make?"

"Shh," he said, pulling her closer. "Don't let that get around."

* * * * *

If you enjoyed this story,
be sure to check out Allie Pleiter's miniseries
Matrimony Valley

His Surprise Son
Snowbound with the Best Man
Wander Canyon Courtship

Find these and other great reads at
www.LoveInspired.com

Dear Reader,

I love a good redemption story, don't you?

It fuels our hope in a better future and the power of grace. When I discovered the Carousel of Happiness in Nederland, Colorado, I knew I had the beginnings of a wonderful, whimsical story. It was the perfect backdrop for a rebel like Wyatt to find a transforming love.

It's often hard to remember that God promises to bring beauty out of ashes. It's challenging to trust a path that bends beyond where you can see, or hold fast to your faith when events seem to spin out of your control. I hope this story reminds you that all the hurdles in your life are never above God's ability to lift you higher.

And if it gets you to take a ride next time you encounter a carousel, well, all the better.

You'll be delighted to know we'll spend two more books in Wander Canyon, meeting its residents and discovering how love changes lives.

As always, I love to hear from you. You can find me on Instagram, Facebook and Twitter, or email me at allie@alliepleiter.com or send a letter to P.O. Box 7026 Villa Park, IL 60181.

Blessings,

WE HOPE YOU ENJOYED
THIS BOOK FROM

LOVE INSPIRED
INSPIRATIONAL ROMANCE

Uplifting stories of faith, forgiveness and hope.

Fall in love with stories where faith helps
guide you through life's challenges, and discover
the promise of a new beginning.

6 NEW BOOKS AVAILABLE EVERY MONTH!

Clang, clang, clang.

The hammering outside her new schoolhouse grew louder. Eva Coblentz moved to the window to locate the source of the clatter. Across the road she saw a man pounding on an ancient-looking piece of machinery with steel wheels and a scoop-like nose on the front end.

When he had the sheet of metal shaped to fit the front of the machine, he stood back to assess his work. He knelt and hammered on the shovel-like nose three more times. Satisfied, he gathered up his tools and started in her direction.

She stepped back from the window. Was he coming to the school? Why? Had he noticed her gawking? Perhaps he only wanted to welcome the new teacher, although his lack of a beard said he wasn't married.

She glanced around the room. Should she meet him by the door? That seemed too eager. Her eyes settled on the large desk at the front of the classroom. She should look as if she was ready for the school year to start. A professional attitude would put off any suggestion that she was interested in meeting single men.

Eva hurried to the desk, pulled out the chair and sat down as the outside door opened. The chair tipped over backward, sending her flailing. Her head hit the wall with a painful thud as she slid to the floor. Stunned, she slowly opened her eyes to see the man leaning over the desk.

He had the most beautiful gray eyes she'd ever beheld. They were rimmed with thick, dark lashes in stark contrast to the mop of curly, dark red hair springing out from beneath his straw hat. Tiny sparks of light whirled around him.

"I'm Willis Gingrich. Local blacksmith." He squatted beside her. "Can you tell me your name?"

The warmth and strength of his hand on her skin sent a sizzle of awareness along her nerve endings. "I'm Eva Coblentz. I am the new teacher and I'm fine now."

Don't miss
The Amish Teacher's Dilemma
by USA TODAY *bestselling author Patricia Davids,*
available March 2020 wherever
Love Inspired books and ebooks are sold.

LoveInspired.com

LIEXP0220

Get 4 FREE REWARDS!

We'll send you 2 FREE Books plus 2 FREE Mystery Gifts.

Love Inspired books feature uplifting stories where faith helps guide you through life's challenges and discover the promise of a new beginning.

FREE Value Over **$20**
